Edith Wharton's

THE HOUSE
OF MIRTH

Adapted for the stage by
Dawn Keeler

A Samuel French Acting Edition

SAMUEL
FRENCH

FOUNDED 1830

New York Hollywood London Toronto

SAMUELFRENCH.COM

ISBN   978-0-573-69573-5   Printed   in   U.S.A.   #10695

IMPORTANT BILLING AND CREDIT REQUIREMENTS

The first performance of this version of
Edith Wharton's
THE HOUSE OF MIRTH
was presented by Cambridge Theatre Company
on 26th April 1995 at the Theatre Royal, Winchester, England
and then toured for nine weeks.

———————————————— **CAST** ————————————————

LILY BART ....Jane Maud
LAWRENCE SELDEN............................. Andrew Hawkins
GERTY FARISH ....Gillian Wright
SIMON ROSEDALE ....Stefan Escreet
JUDY TRENOR ....Ann Firbank
GUS TRENOR ....Carl Forgione
BERTHA DORSET ....Lucinda Curtis
GEORGE DORSET ....Jonathan Lermit
CARRY FISHER ....Seretta Wilson
PERCY GRYCE ....Daniel Stewart

This adaptation was done with the collaboration of
Annie Castledine and Adolf Wood.

LILY BART - 29 year-old, society beauty

LAWRENCE SELDEN - Lawyer in his 30's

GERTY FARISH - Selden's cousin,a spinster in her 30's

SIMON ROSEDALE - Wealthy businessman, 30-40

JUDY TRENOR - Old New York, very wealthy, 40-50

GUS TRENOR - Judy Trenor's financier husband, 45-55

BERTHA DORSET - Small, very pretty socialite, 30-40

GEORGE DORSET - Bertha Dorset's husband, 40-50

CARRY FISHER - Twice divorced, 30-40

PERCY GRYCE - Very wealthy collector, 25-35

Porter

—————————————SETTING————————
The Grand Central Station, New York.

—————————————TIME————————
The play takes place in the present, 1905, and
in the past, 1903 - 1904.
Sometimes the past and present overlap.

ACT I

(MUSIC - Gottschalk's "Suis Moi".)

(ON SCREEN as audience come in. Lights up on sampler on back wall with quotation: "The heart of the wise is in the house of mourning; but the heart of fools is in the house of mirth". — Ecclesiastes, 7.v.4.)

(ON SCREEN, Newspaper Print. Town Talk. New York, May 16, 1905. The funeral of Miss Lily Bart, famed social beauty, who died May 12th, at age 31, takes place today at the Gus Trenors' country estate, Bellomont. A special train will take the coffin and mourners from the Grand Central Station at 10am.)

(SILENCE. Music played very softly on a saxophone. Smoke throughout the opening. LILY BART'S coffin with a spray of lilies is brought on by GUS TRENOR, LAWRENCE SELDEN, SIMON ROSEDALE and GEORGE DORSET. They walk slowly and place it carefully downstage. JUDY TRENOR, BERTHA DORSET, CARRY FISHER, GERTY FARISH and PERCY GRYCE all watch from the top of the stairs. LILY BART comes through the smoke and looks at them all. They cannot see her. JUDY leads the group down the stairs to the coffin. GERTY joins SELDEN looking at the coffin. LILY touches SELDEN lightly on the arm. He shivers and moves away from the group and lights a cigarette.

LILY disappears in the smoke.)

JUDY. How long do we have to wait for this train, Gus? I have an appointment with Celeste this afternoon. I am meeting with Maria Van Osburgh to discuss our autumn wardrobe.

GUS. The train will be here at ten o'clock, Judy.

BERTHA. I, too, have an appointment, you know--with Paquin. I don't understand why Lily is being buried at Bellomont, anyway.

JUDY. Gus insisted, Bertha. For once he seemed quite adamant, so I gave in.

PERCY. Do you think I will need my overshoes, Mrs. Fisher? I never go anywhere without them, you know. But I could leave them in the left luggage if you think...

CARRY. Oh, be daring, Percy. Leave them behind for once.

GERTY. You look very pale, Lawrence. When I saw your face just now, it was as though you'd entered another world. Are you all right? Would you like to sit down? There's still a longish wait before the train comes.

SELDEN. I'm fine, thank you, Gerty dear. I was remembering things...

GERTY. What things?

SELDEN. Two years ago I met Lily, quite accidentally, here at Grand Central Station. I had never seen her more radiant. Everything about her was vibrant and alive. I couldn't believe she was twenty-nine. It occurred to me that she must have cost a great deal to make, and that a great many dull and ugly people must have been sacrificed to produce her. I wondered what she was doing in New York--why she wasn't summering in Newport or Rhode Island. It was characteristic of her to always arouse speculation. I took luxurious pleasure in seeing her again, but wondered what she was up to?

(Station starts to come to life. MUSIC: Gottschalk's "Manchega".)

(ON SCREEN: Grand Central Station New York. Monday, Sept. 16th, 1903. Noise of trains shunting and more steam being let off.)

ANNOUNCEMENT. The train arriving on track two is the 3:30 from Tuxedo.

(Sound of brakes squeaking. Lots of smoke. Through the smoke LILY BART emerges at the top of the stairs looking radiant. She is wearing beautiful clothes, including a delicious hat and carries a parasol. She stands, looking around. She doesn't seem to be in any particular hurry. She sees LAWRENCE SELDEN.)

LILY. Lawrence Selden--what good luck! How nice of you to come to my rescue!

SELDEN. But Miss Bart, surely you know that's my mission in life! May I ask what form the rescue is to take?

LILY. Oh, almost any--even to sitting on a bench and talking to me. One sits out a quadrille--why not sit out a train?

SELDEN. Indeed. But what are you doing in New York at this time of year, Lily? Shouldn't you be in the country?

LILY. I'm on my way from Tuxedo to the Gus Trenors' house party at Bellomont. I've missed the three-fifteen train and there isn't another until half-past five. *(She looks at her little jewelled watch.)* Two hours to wait, and I don't know what to do with myself.

SELDEN. Are you traveling alone?

LILY. Yes. I've sent my maid ahead with all my luggage.

SELDEN. Why don't you go back to your aunt's house, and wait in the cool? I take it you're still living with Mrs. Peniston?

LILY. Her house is closed for the summer. What are *you* doing here, Lawrence?

SELDEN. I'm on my way back to the office. I've been staying a few days with friends in the country.

LILY. *(Fans herself.)* My goodness, it's hot here. If you can spare the time, do take me somewhere for a breath of air.

SELDEN. I'm entirely at your disposal. Shall we go over to Sherry's for a cup of tea?

LILY. *(She pulls a face.)* So many people come up to town on a Monday--one is sure to meet a lot of bores there. I'm dying for tea--but don't you know of a quieter place?

SELDEN. The resources of New York are rather meagre. But we'll invent something.

LILY. How delicious! Let us walk a little. *(She puts up her parasol and takes a walk. As they walk the sound of hansom cabs and the occasional motor hooter are heard.)* What a hideous city this is! Other cities put on their best clothes in summer, but New York seems to sit in its shirt-sleeves. Oh look, some one has had the humanity to plant a few trees over there.

SELDEN. I am glad my street meets with your approval.

LILY. Your street? Do you live here?

SELDEN. Yes.

LILY. *The Benedick.* What a nice looking building! I don't think I've ever seen it before. Which are your windows?

SELDEN. Those with the awnings down. On the top floor.

LILY. And that nice little balcony is yours, too?

SELDEN. Yes.

LILY. How cool it looks up there!

SELDEN. Come up and see. I can give you a cup of tea in no time--and you won't meet any bores.

LILY. *(Pause.)* Oh, why not? It's too tempting--I'll take the risk.

(LILY pauses at the top of the stairs.)

SELDEN. I'm not dangerous. There's no one there, and it's just possible my servant may have put out the tea-things and provided some cake.

LILY. How delicious to have a place like this all to one's self! What a miserable thing it is to be a woman!

SELDEN. Why? Even women have been known to enjoy the privileges of a flat.

LILY. Oh, governesses--or widows. But not girls--not poor, miserable, marriageable girls!

SELDEN. I even know a girl who lives in a flat.

LILY. You do?

SELDEN. I do.

(A PORTER--in present reality--followed by GERTY FARISH, who tips him, enters with tea-things and a cake.)

LILY. You mean Gerty Farish. But I said *marriageable*-- and besides, she has a horrid little place, and no maid, and such queer things to eat. Her cook does the washing and the food tastes of soap. I should hate that, you know.

SELDEN. *(He cuts the cake.)* You shouldn't dine with her on wash days.

LILY. It was horrid of me to say that of Gerty. I forgot she was your cousin. But we're so different, you know: and besides, she is free and I am not. If I were, I daresay I could manage to be happy even in her flat. It must be pure bliss to arrange the furniture just as one likes. If I could only do over my aunt's drawing-room I know I should be a better woman.

SELDEN. Is it so very bad?

LILY. That shows how seldom you come there. Why don't you come more often?

SELDEN. When I do come it's not to look at Mrs. Peniston's furniture.

LILY. Nonsense, you don't come at all--and yet we get on so well when we meet.

SELDEN. Perhaps that's the reason. I'm afraid I haven't any cream, shall you mind a slice of lemon instead?

LILY. I shall like it better. But that is not the reason.

SELDEN. The reason for what?

(SELDEN hands LILY her tea.)

LILY. For your never coming. I wish I could make you out. I know there are men who don't like me--and there are others who are afraid I want to marry them. But I don't think you dislike me--and you can't possibly think I want to marry you.

SELDEN. Well, then—

(SELDEN drinks his tea, observing LILY closely.)

SELDEN. Well, then, perhaps *that's* the reason.

LILY. What?

SELDEN. The fact that you don't want to marry me. Perhaps

I don't regard it as such a strong inducement to go and see you.

LILY. Dear Lawrence, that wasn't worthy of you. It's stupid of you to try and make love to me, and it isn't like you to be stupid. *(She sips her tea.)* Don't you see, that there are men enough to say pleasant things to me, but what I want is a friend who won't be afraid to say disagreeable ones when I need them? Sometimes I have fancied you might be that friend.

SELDEN. Why me?

LILY. I don't know why, except that you are neither a prig nor a bounder, and that I shouldn't have to pretend with you or be on my guard against you. You don't know how much I need such a friend. My best friends use me or abuse me, but they don't care a straw what happens to me. I've been about too long--people are getting tired of me; they are beginning to say I ought to marry.

SELDEN. Well, why don't you?

LILY. Ah, I see you *are* a friend after all, and that is one of the disagreeable things I was asking for.

SELDEN. It wasn't meant to be disagreeable. Isn't marriage your vocation? Isn't it what you're all brought up for?

LILY. *(Sighs.)* I suppose so. What else is there?

SELDEN. Exactly. So why not take the plunge and have it over?

LILY. You speak as though I ought to marry the first man who came along.

SELDEN. I didn't mean to imply that you are as hard put to it as that. But there must be some one with the requisite qualifications.

LILY. Not really. You know I am horribly poor--and very expensive. I must have a great deal of money.

SELDEN. But surely you will inherit your aunt's fortune.

LILY. I have been led to believe so, but I can't bank on it.

SELDEN. *(Takes a cigarette out of his case.)* What's become of Dillworth?

LILY. His mother was afraid I should have all the family jewels reset. And she wanted me to promise that I wouldn't do over the drawing-room.

SELDEN. The very thing you are marrying for!

LILY. Exactly. So she packed him off to India.

SELDEN. Hard luck--but you can do better than Dillworth.

(SELDEN offers LILY a cigarette.)

LILY. Have I time? Just a whiff then. *(She takes three or four cigarettes, puts one in her mouth and the rest in a gold case attached to her pearl chain. She leans forward and lights her cigarette from SELDEN'S. Their eyes meet. She gets up and starts wandering around the room looking at the books.)* You collect, don't you--you know about first editions and things?

SELDEN. As much as a man may who has no money to spend. Now and then I pick up something in the rubbish heap; and I go round the big sales.

LILY. And Americana--do you collect Americana?

SELDEN. *(Laughing.)* No, that's rather out of my line. I'm not really a collector, you see; I simply like to have good editions of the books I'm fond of.

LILY. And Americana must be horribly dull, I suppose?

SELDEN. I should fancy so--except to the historian. I don't suppose that buyers of Americana sit up reading them all night-- Percy Gryce's uncle, old Jefferson Gryce, certainly didn't.

LILY. Is it true that his collection of Americana is considered the most valuable in the world?

SELDEN. I believe so.

LILY. How did he make his fortune?

SELDEN. Out of a patent device for excluding fresh air from hotels!

LILY. If you were a collector of Americana, what particular things would you want to buy?

(LILY continues to take books out of the shelves, fluttering the pages between her fingers.)

SELDEN. Oh, I don't know. News sheets printed in the 17th century. Rare first editions, Benjamin Franklin's letters, private diaries, things like that.

LILY. What do you suppose would be the most valuable item to own?

SELDEN. Probably Columbus's Letter on his First Voyage. But why all this interest in Americana? Are *you* thinking of becoming a collector?

LILY. No, no--just curious. Don't you ever mind not being rich enough to buy all the books you want?

SELDEN. Don't I just? Do you take me for a saint on a pillar?

LILY. And having to work--do you mind that?

SELDEN. Actually, I'm rather fond of the law.

LILY. But the being tied down: the routine--don't you ever want to get away?

SELDEN. Horribly--especially when I see all my friends rushing off to ocean liners.

SELDEN. But you don't mind enough--to marry to get out of it?

SELDEN. God forbid!

LILY. Ah, there's the difference--a girl must, a man may if he chooses. Your coat's a little shabby--but who cares? It doesn't keep people from asking you to dine. If I were shabby no one would have me: who wants a dingy woman? We are expected to be pretty and well-dressed till we drop--and if we can't keep it up alone, we have to go into partnership.

SELDEN. Perhaps you'll meet your fate tonight at the Trenors'.

LILY. I thought you might be going.,

SELDEN. Judy Trenor asked me; but those big parties bore me.

LILY. So they do me.

SELDEN. Then why go?

LILY. It's part of the business--you forget! Besides, if I didn't, I should be playing bézique with my aunt at Richfield Springs.

SELDEN. That's almost as bad as marrying Dillworth.

(They both laugh, sharing a moment of intimacy. LILY glances at the clock.)

LILY. Dear me! I must be off. It's after five. *(She looks in the mirror, and adjusts her veil after studying herself. She holds out her hand to SELDEN.)* It's been delightful; and now you will have to return my visit.

SELDEN. But don't you want me to see you to the station?

LILY. No; good-bye here, please, Lawrence.

SELDEN. Goodbye, then, Lily, and good luck at Bellomont!

SELDEN and LILY are still holding hands. PERCY, carrying

a newspaper, goes up to SELDEN.)

PERCY. Would you like me to stay with the coffin for a while? I'm quite happy to...

(SELDEN reluctantly lets go of LILY'S hand and turns away.)

SELDEN. No, it's all right... Thank you.

(LILY goes up the stairs and watches. PERCY opens his newspaper.)

ROSEDALE. I don't wonder you're upset, Selden. You of all people could have saved her from this. I bumped into her, you know, leaving the Benedick on her way to a Bellomont house-party, in the days before I was invited there, of course-- I saw her leaving your flat.

SELDEN. And I've no doubt you kept that knowledge entirely to yourself.

ROSEDALE. I'm not saying I'm blameless. But that wasn't the only thing I saw.

SELDEN. What are you talking about?

ROSEDALE. Mrs. Haffen--you remember her, Selden? The charwoman who used to clean your rooms? She was scrubbing the stairs when Lily came out of your flat. I recall that Lily had to gather up her skirts to get by her.

LILY. **Could one never do the simplest, the most harmless thing without subjecting oneself to some odious conjecture? I thought I had escaped her gaze when...**

ROSEDALE. Just as Lily reached the bottom stair, Mrs. Haffen called out to her. Lily stopped--Mrs. Haffen brought out a bundle of letters from her pocket--about a dozen or so, as far as I could see, they looked as though they had been torn in half and put together again. After quite a discussion, I saw Lily reach in her purse and give Mrs. Haffen a handful of dollar bills.

LILY. *(She takes the letters out of her bag.)* **Mrs. Haffen supposed me to be the writer of the letters, and she was trying to blackmail me. They were addressed to you, Lawrence, in Bertha Dorset's large, disjointed hand. I thought your affair was over, and judging from the pleading nature of the contents, for you it was. The momentary triumph I felt at having some power over you, Bertha, gave way to a feeling of contamination and disgust. I had no idea what I was going to do with the letters, only that I must get them away from Mrs. Haffen, who was threatening to take them to the news...**

(Before LILY can finish her sentence SIMON ROSEDALE steps forward. He raises his hat.)

ROSEDALE. Miss Bart? Well--of all people! This *is* luck.

(LILY puts the bundle of letters in her bag, ROSEDALE sees this.)

LILY. Oh, Mr. Rosedale--how are you?
ROSEDALE. *(Looking up at the porch of the Benedick.)* Been up to town for a little shopping, I suppose?
LILY. Yes--I came up to see my dress-maker. I am just on my way to catch the train to the Trenors'. I'm afraid I'm in a great hurry.

ROSEDALE. Ah--your dress-maker; I see. I didn't know there were any dress-makers in the Benedick.

LILY. The Benedick? Is that the name of this building?

ROSEDALE. Yes, that's the name: I believe it's an old word for bachelor, isn't it? I happen to own the building--that's how I know. But you must let me take you to the station. The Trenors are at Bellomont, of course? You've barely time to catch the five-forty. The dress-maker kept you waiting I suppose.

LILY. *(Embarrassed.)* Thank you, you're very kind; but I couldn't think of troubling you.

BERTHA. If I'd known we were going to have to wait this long, I would have brought some cards with me.

GEORGE. Why don't you try reading some poetry instead?

CARRY. Now, now, George!

JUDY. If I don't get to Celeste's before Maria Van Osburgh, she'll pick all the best designs.

GUS. Oh, do stop fussing, Judy. Don't you ever think of anything except spending my money?

(MUSIC: Gottschalk's "Manchega".)

STATION ANNOUNCEMENT. The nine-forty-five train to Rhinebeck is leaving from track three in four minutes. Will passengers for this train please board now.

(PERCY looks up from his newspaper when he hears the announcement.)

BERTHA. Rhinebeck! Do you remember, Percy, I met you on that train with Lily, going to Bellomont.

PERCY. I shall never forget it, Mrs. Dorset.

(Sounds of steam being let off. LILY arranges herself beauti-
fully, looks at her reflection, adjusts her hat, and takes out
a new book. She starts to cut the pages. Both LILY and
PERCY pretend not to see each other. He hides behind his
newspaper. LILY gets up and walks down the carriage and
as she draws alongside PERCY the train lurches and she
puts out her hand to steady herself on PERCY'S seat. He
jumps up, acutely embarrassed. The train lurches again,
almost throwing LILY into PERCY'S arms.)

LILY. Oh, Mr. Gryce, I'm so sorry--I was trying to find
where the porter is with my tea. Are you by any chance going
to Bellomont?

PERCY. Yes, I am. I heard that you were to be one of the
party. I am invited for the whole week.

LILY. How delightful! *(She sees the PORTER.)* Ah! Here's
my tea now. *(She goes back to her seat calling over her shoul-*
der.) The chair next to mine is empty--do take it. *(The POR-*
TER puts a tray in front of LILY.) Porter, bring another cup
please. *(PERCY gets up with all his baggage and joins LILY.*
The PORTER brings another cup. She pours the tea elegantly
while PERCY watches. She hands him a cup and smiles at
him.) I hope I haven't made it too strong.

PERCY. *(Flustered.)* It's the best tea I've ever tasted.

(An awkward silence.)

LILY. I met your mother the other day at my aunt's.

PERCY. Oh, yes.

LILY. She's been having trouble with the servants again, I
believe.

PERCY. Yes.

LILY. Kitchen-maids smuggling groceries out of the house.

PERCY. Yes.

(Another awkward silence. Smoke from cigarettes wafts past PERCY'S face, and he fans the air.)

LILY. You don't smoke, Mr. Gryce?

PERCY. Oh, no, Miss Bart. I would never let tobacco defile my lips.

(Silence.)

LILY. And how are you getting on with your Americana?

PERCY. *(Suddenly galvanized.)* Oh, you know about my--er--passion? I've got a few new things.

LILY. Oh, do tell me about them.

PERCY. *(Lowers his voice for fear of being overheard.)* Well, my most recent purchase is a beautiful first edition of Emerson's essays.

LILY. How clever of you to find that.

PERCY. Yes, and the really exciting thing is that it's an autographed copy.

LILY. Well I never! I suppose you collect 17th-century news sheets, diaries and suchlike.

PERCY. Oh, yes! You must let me show you my private library one day.

LILY. Have you ever seen Columbus's Letter on his First Voyage?

PERCY. *(Impressed.)* Oh, yes, to be sure. The Columbus Letter is the first of all Americana. It's one of the treasures of the New York Public Library. I spend hours there every week. They also have a copy of the first illustrated Latin edition, printed in Basle.

LILY. Oh, Mr. Gryce, you are so knowledgeable!

PERCY. *(Now in full swing.)* Another of the finest collections of Americana, apart from mine of course, is in the John Carter Brown Library in Providence.

(The PORTER comes and removes the tea tray.)

LILY. I suppose you know about the collections in all the libraries?

PERCY. Oh, yes. The Newberry Library in Chicago, the Huntington in San Marino, the Clements Library in Ann Arbor, Michigan, the...

(PERCY is interrupted by BERTHA DORSET, causing a commotion.)

BERTHA. Oh, Lily--are you going to Bellomont? I must have a seat in this carriage--porter, you must find me a place at once. Can't some one be put somewhere else? I want to be with my friends. Oh, how do you do, Mr. Gryce? Do please make him understand that I must have a seat next to you and Lily. *(The PORTER clears a seat for her next to LILY and she finally settles down.)* I came across from Mount Kisco this morning in my motor-car, and have been kicking my heels for an hour at Garrisons, without even a cigarette. That stupid George forgot to replenish my case this morning, and I don't suppose at this hour of the day you've a single one left, have you, Lily?

(PERCY looks startled.)

LILY. What an absurd question, Bertha!

BERTHA. Why, you smoke, don't you? *(LILY gives her a look.)* Since when have you given it up?

LILY. I've never—

BERTHA. What--you never--And you don't either, Mr. Gryce? Ah, of course--how stupid of me--I understand.

(BERTHA starts to laugh.)

GEORGE. Bertha, stop it. You are making a spectacle of yourself.

BERTHA. I can't help it. I suddenly saw how ridiculous we all look. Dressed in black, like a lot of crows. We should be going to one of your house-parties, Judy, not Lily Bart's funeral.

(The sound of a roulette wheel. Waltz music: Joseph Lanner's "Vermählungs-Waltzer".)

JUDY. Pragg has just telephoned to say she is not coming in for a few days. Her sister is having a baby--as if that were anything to having a house-party. It's simply inhuman of her to go off now. Lily, if it's not a bore, will you come and help me? There are all the dinner cards to write, and addresses to hunt up. When I was down at Tuxedo I asked a lot of people for next week, and I've mislaid the list. I can't remember who's staying on this week, and how many I've invited to come on Thursday. It really is too tiresome. I know this week is going to be a horrid failure too--and Gwen Van Osburgh will go back and tell her mother how bored people were.

LILY. Oh, Judy--as if anyone were ever bored at Bellomont.

JUDY. Now, dear, let's get started. *(LILY is ready with pen and paper.)* I know the Wetheralls are staying until next Friday. That was a blunder of Gus's. They can stay in the Peacock Room.

LILY. *(She writes down the Wetheralls name and room.)* What was Gus's blunder?

JUDY. They disapprove of Carry Fisher. It *was* foolish of her to get the second divorce--Carry always overdoes things. But she's the only person who can keep Gus in a good humor when we have bores in the house, and even though I know she borrows money from him, I'd pay her to do that. I've just remembered! I invited Audrey Anstell. She is staying with the Dick Bellingers and they asked if they could bring her with them. Such a mousey little creature, but she plays a formidable game of bridge.

(MUSIC in next room changes to Gottschalk's Polka in Bb.)

LILY. She can have my room then, and the Bellingers can go in the Oriental Room. *(Without looking up from her writing.)* Carry borrows money from Gus?

JUDY. Yes. It's rather clever of her to have made a specialty of devoting herself to dull people, and quite lucrative too. Gwen and Evie Van Osburgh are staying on for a few days. Gwen and Jack Stepney are getting on so well, I shouldn't be surprised if they announce their engagement. Where have we got to?

LILY. *(She refers to her list.)* The Wetheralls, the Van Osburgh girls and Jack are all staying on, and so far we have

Audrey Anstell, and the Dick Bellingers arriving on
Thursday. When is Lady Cressida Raith leaving?

JUDY. *(She laughs.)* My dear, if only one knew! I was in
such a hurry to get her away from Maria Van Osburgh that I
actually forgot to name a date. If I'd known what she was like,
they could have had her and welcome.

LILY. Hadn't you known her before?

JUDY. Mercy, no--never saw her till yesterday. She's the
Duchess of Beltshire's sister, and I naturally supposed she was
the same sort; but you never can tell in those English families.

LILY. Which room is she in?

JUDY. The garden room. I thought it would remind her of
home! I know there's some one else. Give me a cigarette, dear,
and perhaps it will come to me. *(LILY holds out her cigarette
case and JUDY takes one. LILY lights it for her. Laughter and
clapping from the next room.)* I'm sorry, dear, to keep you from
the dancing. By the way, Bertha will be furious with me.

LILY. Furious with you? Why?

JUDY. Because I told her Lawrence Selden was coming,
and he isn't after all and she will think it's all my fault.

LILY. I thought it was all over between them.

JUDY. So it is, on his side. I suppose she'll take it out on
me by being perfectly nasty to everyone else.

LILY. Or she may take it out on *him* by being perfectly
charming--to some one else.

JUDY. She knows he wouldn't mind. And who else is there?
Ned Silverton's too young. Gus is bored by her, and Jack
Stepney knows her too well--and-- well, there's Percy Gryce!

LILY. Oh, she wouldn't be likely to hit it off with him.

JUDY. I hope she won't be nice to him, because I asked
him here on purpose for you.

LILY. *Merci du compliment*! I should certainly have no show against Bertha.

JUDY. Everyone knows you're a thousand times handsomer and cleverer than Bertha; but then you're not nasty.

LILY. I thought you were so fond of Bertha.

JUDY. Oh, I am--it's much safer to be fond of dangerous people. And she *is* dangerous. If ever I saw her up to mischief it's now. I can tell by poor George's manner--he always knows when Bertha is going to—

LILY. To fall?

JUDY. Don't be shocking! You know he believes in her still, only she delights in making people miserable, especially poor George.

LILY. Well, he seems cut out for the part--I don't wonder she likes more cheerful companionship.

JUDY. George is not as dismal as you think. If Bertha would leave him alone, he'd be quite different, but she doesn't dare lose her hold of him on account of the money, and so when *he* isn't jealous she pretends to be. I've just remembered who it is I invited. The Ned Wintons. Both of them on their second marriages, you know.

LILY. Where would you like me to put them?

(The polka ends. Everyone claps.)

JUDY. I guess you'd better put them in the Japanese Room. It has the best view of the lake. Do you know I believe I will telephone Lawrence and tell him he simply *must* come.

LILY. *(Hurriedly.)* Oh, don't.

JUDY. Good gracious, Lily, you're blushing!--Why? Do you dislike him so much?

LILY. Not at all; I like him. But I don't think I need to be protected from Bertha.

JUDY. Lily!--*Percy*? Do you mean to say you've actually done it?

LILY. I only mean to say that Mr. Gryce and I are getting to be good friends.

(MUSIC: Viennese Waltz. Joseph Lanner's "Abendsterne".)

JUDY. You know, they say he has eight hundred thousand a year--and spends nothing, except on rubbishy old books. *Oh, Lily, do go slowly.*

LILY. I shouldn't be in haste to tell him that he had a lot of rubbishy old books.

JUDY. No, of course not; I know you are wonderful about getting up people's subjects. But he's horribly shy, and easily shocked, and—

LILY. Why don't you say it, Judy? I have a reputation of being on the hunt for a rich husband.

JUDY. I don't mean that; but don't wear your scarlet crêpe-de-chine, and don't smoke if you can help it, Lily dear!

LILY. I'll lock up my cigarettes and wear that last year's dress you sent me this morning, and perhaps you'll be kind enough not to ask me to play bridge or roulette again.

JUDY. Does he mind gambling, too? Oh, Lily, what an awful life you'll lead! But of course I won't--why didn't you give me a hint? There's nothing I wouldn't do to see you happy! Is Percy dancing with the others? I hope he doesn't disapprove of that too.

LILY. He said he was going to have an early night. We have arranged to go to church together in the morning.

JUDY. Oh, I see. You're quite sure you wouldn't like me to telephone for Lawrence Selden?

(JUDY moves away from LILY, taking in BERTHA DORSET. Sound of roulette wheel getting louder.)

LILY. Quite sure.

GUS. Come along, ladies and gentlemen, faites vos jeux.

JUDY. Lily, come and play one last game of roulette, while Percy's out of the way!

CARRY. Which charity is the bank going to tonight, Judy?

JUDY. Gerty Farish's Girl's Club.

GUS. Place your bets, ladies and gentlemen.

JUDY. Are you not playing, Carry?

CARRY. No. I lost too much at bridge earlier. I'll be the bank. *(GUS offers her a cigarette, which she takes, and he lights it for her.)* By the way, where are Jack and Gwen?

BERTHA. Last seen, holding hands in the conservatory.

CARRY. When are they announcing their engagement?

JUDY. Very soon now, I gather. Gwen wants to get married in November.

BERTHA. And of course Jack'll have Simon Rosedale as his best man. Gus, place these chips on 36 for me will you? You might bring me luck.

GUS. Jove, that's an idea. What a thumping present they'd get out of him! Cigar? *(GUS offers a cigar to GEORGE who takes one.)* I must remember to thank him for introducing me to Simon Rosedale. I did a very neat stroke of business yesterday, with his help. *(Raising his voice.)* I wish I could persuade Judy to ask him to Bellomont. He's going to be rich enough to buy us all out one of these days. *(GUS spins the wheel.)* No more bets. She objects to him because he's Jewish, you know. He's been rejected a dozen times by the social board, and she won't hear of even being civil to him. Rien ne va plus. *(EVERYONE stops talking and watches as the ball settles.)* Seize rouge. *(GUS holds the chips on 16 Red with a dolly and clears the rest of the table.)*

BERTHA. You have the luck of the devil, Judy!

GUS. You won't need my money at this rate! *(GUS pushes the chips towards JUDY. She piles them up in front of her.)* Faites vos jeux, please. *(Still carrying on the conversation with GEORGE.)* If she'd only ask Simon Rosedale to dine now and then I could get almost anything out of him. A few years from now he'll be in whether we want him or not and then he won't be giving away a half-a-million tip for a dinner.

GEORGE. No he won't, and who can blame him?

(JUDY puts a pile of chips on, LILY only has two chips left. She places them on the red mark. BERTHA places hers on the same number as JUDY.)

BERTHA. I thought Ned was coming to play. I suppose he's got his head stuck in a poetry book. *(She starts to recite.)*
"Je fais souvent ce rêve étrange et pénétrant
D'une femme inconnue, et que j'aime, et qui m'aime,
Et qui n'est, chaque fois, ni tout à fait la même
Ni tout à fait une autre, et m'aime et me comprend."
Paul Verlaine!

GUS. Very impressive, Bertha. I didn't know you liked poetry--let alone French poetry!

BERTHA. That's because you don't know me very well.

GUS. *(Spinning the wheel.)* No more bets. He'll be wanting

to show you his sonnets, next.

BERTHA. If he writes poetry, I shall certainly encourage
him.

*(They ALL watch the wheel as it slows down. The ball settles
on JUDY'S number again.)*

GUS. Dix-sept noir. 17 Black. *(JUDY and BERTHA let out
whoops of delight, and wait for GUS to push their chips over.)*
This is getting embarrassing. People will think we've fixed
the wheel.

*(LILY watches hers taken away with growing alarm. JUDY
now has several piles of chips in front of her.)*

BERTHA. Never mind, Lily, better luck next time.

GEORGE. *(Jokingly. To LILY.)* My wife is making a fool
of herself with Ned Silverton. One would really suppose she
was gone on him--and it's all the other way round, I assure
you.

LILY. Aren't you horribly jealous of her?

GEORGE. Oh, abominably--you've just hit it--keeps me
awake at night. The doctors tell me that's what has knocked
my digestion out. That and these fancy new chefs. I cannot
understand why fish has to be served with a sauce, nowadays.
I always scrape it off. And everything is swimming in melted
butter. Do you know how toxic melted butter is? I dread these
house-parties. The cooks are always so inferior to ours, and I
end up with chronic dyspepsia.

GUS. Ladies and gentlemen, a little less chat. Place your
bets, please.

BERTHA. Did Lily tell you I met her on the train with Percy Gryce?

JUDY. Yes, she did mention it.

BERTHA. When I asked her for a cigarette, she pretended she didn't smoke. Would you believe it?

(LILY looks uncomfortable as they ALL laugh.)

JUDY. *(Placing a huge pile of chips on the table.)* Lily, take these, and have one more go. You can pay me back later.

(LILY takes the chips and places them on the table.)

CARRY. My dear, where *did* you find Lady Cressida Raith?

JUDY. You may well ask!

BERTHA. Place those on rouge for me, Gus dear.

JUDY. I've never met her before. Serves me right though.

CARRY. Why?

JUDY. She was supposed to be staying with the Van Osburghs, and I thought it would be fun to get her away.

GUS. She's married to a clergyman and does missionary work in the East End of London.

BERTHA. How can you be bothered with a clergyman's wife who wears Indian jewelry and botanizes?

JUDY. *(Laughing.)* She made Gus take her all through the glasshouses yesterday, and bothered him to death by asking him the names of the plants.

CARRY. Fancy treating Gus as if he were the gardener!

BERTHA. When is she leaving?

GUS. She intends to stop here all winter.

CARRY. In this house?

GUS. Don't be silly--in America. But if no one else asks her--you know the English *never* go to hotels. Rien ne va plus.

(GUS spins the wheel.)

JUDY. She would have been so useful last year when we had the Bishop here...

GUS. *(Laughing.)* Oh, yes. That's when I forgot he was here and brought back the Ned Wintons and the Farleys, five divorces and six sets of children between them!

(They ALL laugh. The wheel starts to slow down. LILY is watching it anxiously. The ball settles.)

GUS. 13 black.

(He scoops up all the chips except JUDY'S again. He pushes a huge pile over to her. JUDY starts to count them while LILY looks on.)

JUDY. I think perhaps we should call it a day. It's after midnight, and I don't want our other guests to think we gamble on Sundays. Poor Lily, you're not having much luck lately. Carry, change my chips for me, will you?

(LILY looks inside her bag. It is empty.)

LILY. I will settle with you tomorrow.

LILY leaves the others and goes up the stairs. SELDEN walks around the upper level of the station. He sees LILY and looks down at the others.)

SELDEN. You see I came after all.

(JUDY gets up from the table clutching a heap of bills.)

JUDY. Lawrence, how lovely! *(She kisses him.)* Why didn't you telephone me, I would have sent the trap for you? *(They ALL gather around SELDEN shaking his hand.)* Well, I was just on my way to bed so I'll say good night.

(JUDY exits to a chorus of good night, and everyone else goes except LILY and BERTHA.)

SELDEN. *(To LILY.)* Take a walk with me in the morning.
LILY. I have another engagement. Perhaps in the afternoon. Good night, Lawrence.

(LILY holds out her hand.)

SELDEN. I must return to New York in the afternoon.
LILY. So soon? I'll see. Good night. *(SELDEN takes LILY'S hand and holds it for a moment. BERTHA moves swiftly to SELDEN'S side and puts a proprietorial hand on his arm. SELDEN turns out of BERTHA'S hold.)* **The world that night seemed a miserable place. I lingered on the stairway looking down into the hall below, where the last of you were grouped about the tray of tall glasses and silver-collared decanters. There were moments when such scenes delighted me, and gratified my sense of beauty; but that night they gave a sharper edge to the meagerness of my own oppor-**

tunities. Surely there was room for me in your crowded selfish world of pleasure. I had almost landed you, Percy-- but you were so boring. You had bored me all afternoon. Did I really want you to do me the honor of boring me for life. But what choice did I have? To be myself, or like you Gerty. As I entered my bedroom with its softly-shaded lights, the fire burning in the hearth, a vase of carnations filling the air with perfume, I had a vision of your cramped flat, Gerty, with its cheap conveniences and hideous wallpapers. I was not made for mean and shabby surroundings, I needed luxury--it was the only atmosphere I could breathe in. But I was getting out of my depth, the gambling passion was upon me, my luck seemed to have deserted me, and that night I lost three hundred dollars. When I went through my accounts I realized my finances were in worse shape than I had imagined--only twenty dollars left. For a moment I thought I had been robbed! I went over the figures again and again, but nothing could conjure back the vanished three hundred dollars. It reminded me of the terrible day my world crashed. I was having luncheon with my mother.

VO LILY. I really think, mother, we might afford a few fresh flowers for luncheon. Just some jonquils, or lilies-of-the-valley—

VO MRS. BART. Lilies-of-the-valley cost two dollars a dozen at this season.

VO LILY. It would not take more than six dozen to fill that bowl.

VO MR. BART. Six dozen what?

VO LILY. I was only saying, father, that I hate to see faded flowers at luncheon; and mother says a bunch of lilies-of-the-

valley would not cost more than twelve dollars. Mayn't I tell
the florist to send a few every day?

VO MR. BART. Twelve dollars a day for flowers? *(He starts laughing.)* Oh, certainly my dear--give him an order for twelve hundred.

(MR. BART continues to laugh, getting more uncontrollable.)

VO MRS. BART. What's the matter, Hudson? Are you ill?

VO MR. BART. Ill? Ill? No, I'm ruined.

VO MRS. BART. Your father is not well--he doesn't
know what he is saying. It is nothing--but you'd better
go upstairs; and don't talk to the servants. You are sorry
for him now--but you will feel differently when you see
what he has done to us. *(Pause.)* Don't let dinginess creep
up on you and drag you down. Fight your way out of it
somehow--you're young and you can do it.

LILY. **My mother's words were ringing in my ears.
"You'll get the money back--you'll get it all back with your
face". My beauty was all that I had and it was fading away.
I returned wearily to the thought of you, Percy--a few more
days' work and I would win my reward--I would have
smarter dresses than you, Judy, and far more jewels than
you, Bertha. Instead of having to flatter I would be flattered. Instead of being grateful, I would receive thanks. I
would be free forever from the humiliation of being poor.
But in return, what a price I would have to pay. Church**
every **Sunday, with you Percy. We would have a front pew
in the most expensive church in New York, and your name
would figure handsomely in the list of parish charities. In
a few years, when you grew stouter, you would be made a
warden. Once a year the rector would come to dine and**

you would make me go over the list to make sure no divorcees were included, except, of course, those who had showed penitence by being married to the very wealthy. At the very least, being married to you would have been a refuge from worry, nothing more. *(Sound of church bells.)* Much to my surprise, I slept well that night, and there was no trace of the little lines I had seen around my mouth. *(LILY admires herself in the mirror. Puts her Omar Khayyam in her pocket. Walks downstairs into bright sunlight. Birds singing.)* I had every intention of going to church with you, Percy, but I lingered too long with my thoughts--thoughts of you, Lawrence. Why had you come to Bellomont after all? Was it to see me or Bertha Dorset? It was a beautiful day--a day for impulse and truancy! Every drop of blood in my veins invited me to happiness.

(LILY puts on her hat, and picks up her parasol, when she catches sight of BERTHA and LAWRENCE talking to each other.)

BERTHA. You never answer my letters, Lawrence--but I forgive you, now that you've come to Bellomont after all. I presume you did come to see me?

LILY. Dear me, am I late?

BERTHA. Late for what? Not for luncheon, certainly--but perhaps you had an earlier engagement?

LILY. Yes, I had.

BERTHA. Really? Perhaps I am in the way, then? But Mr. Selden is entirely at your disposal.

LILY. Oh, dear, no--do stay. I don't in the least want to drive you away.

BERTHA. How nice of you, dear, but I never interfere with Mr. Selden's engagements.

LILY. I have no engagement with Mr. Selden! My engagement was to go to church; but I'm afraid the omnibus has started without me. *Has* it started, do you know?

SELDEN. I heard it leave quite a while ago.

LILY. Then I shall have to walk. I promised the Trenor girls I would go to church with them. At least I shall have the credit of trying, and the advantage of escaping part of the service!

(LILY leaves them and finds a place on the ground and arranges herself elegantly. She takes her Omar Khayyam from her pocket and starts to read it. SELDEN comes up to her. She looks up and sees him.)

SELDEN. How fast you walk! I thought I should never catch up with you.

LILY. You must be quite breathless! I've been sitting under this tree for an hour.

SELDEN. *(He sits on the ground beside her.)* Waiting for me, I hope?

LILY. Well--waiting to see if you would come.

SELDEN. I didn't know you read poetry. *(He takes her Omar Khayyam and looks at it.)* The Rubaiyat of Omar Khayyam.

LILY. I always carry it with me. It was my father's.

SELDEN. *(Not looking at her.)* But weren't you sure that I would come?

LILY. If I waited long enough--but you see I had only a limited time to give the experiment.

SELDEN. Why limited? Limited by luncheon?

LILY. No; by my other engagement.

SELDEN. Your engagement to go to church with the Trenor girls.

LILY. No; but to come home from church with another person.

SELDEN. Percy Gryce, you mean?

LILY. How did you guess?

SELDEN. By putting two and two together. Now I see why you were getting up your Americana!

LILY. That was why I was waiting for you--to thank you for having given me so many points! But why did you change your mind and come to Bellomont after all?

SELDEN. To see you.

LILY. Did you really come to see me?

SELDEN. Of course I did.

LILY. Why?

SELDEN. Because you're such a wonderful spectacle: I always like to see what you are doing.

LILY. How do you know what I should be doing if you were not here?

SELDEN. I don't flatter myself that my coming has deflected your course of action by a hair's breadth

LILY. That's absurd--since, if you were not here, I could obviously not be taking a walk with you.

SELDEN. No; but your taking a walk with me is only another way of making use of your material. You are an artist and I happen to be the bit of color you are using today. It's part of your cleverness to be able to produce premeditated effects extemporaneously.

LILY. I don't know why you are always accusing me of premeditation.

SELDEN. I thought you confessed to it: you told me the other day that you had to follow a certain line.

LILY. You must find me a dismal kind of person if you suppose that I never yield to an impulse.

SELDEN. Ah, but I don't suppose that: haven't I told you that your genius lies in converting impulses into intentions?

LILY. Is there any final test of genius but success? And I certainly haven't succeeded.

SELDEN. Success--what is success? I shall be interested to have your definition.

LILY. To get as much as one can out of life, I suppose. Isn't that your idea of it?

SELDEN. My idea of it? God forbid! My idea of success is personal freedom.

LILY. Freedom? Freedom from worries?

SELDEN. Freedom from everything--from money, from poverty, from ease and anxiety, from all the material accidents. To keep a kind of **republic of the spirit**--that's what I call success.

(Strains of a hymn are heard in the distance.)

LILY. I know--I know--it's what I've been feeling today.

SELDEN. Is the feeling so rare with you?

LILY. You think me horribly sordid, don't you? But there was no one to tell me about the republic of the spirit.

SELDEN. There never is--it's a country one has to find the way to one's self.

LILY. But I should never have found my way there if you hadn't told me.

SELDEN. There are sign-posts--but one has to know how to read them.

LILY. Well, I have known, I have known! Whenever I see you, I find myself spelling out a letter of the sign.

SELDEN. Are you going to become one of us?

(SELDEN takes out a packet of cigarettes.)

LILY. Oh, do give me one--I haven't smoked for hours!

SELDEN. Why such unnatural abstinence? Everybody smokes at Bellomont.

LILY. It is not considered becoming in a *jeune fille à marier,* and at the moment I am a *jeune fille à marier.*

SELDEN. Ah, then I'm afraid we can't let you into the republic. You will marry some one very rich, and it's as hard for rich people to get into as the kingdom of heaven.

LILY. That's unjust, because, as I understand it, one of the conditions of citizenship is not to think too much about money, and the only way not to think about money is to have a great deal of it.

SELDEN. You might as well say that the only way not to think about air is not to breathe, and so it is with your rich people--they may not be thinking of money but they're breathing it all the while; take them into another element and see how they squirm and gasp!

LILY. It seems to me that you spend a good deal of your time in the element you disapprove of.

SELDEN. Good heavens! I don't underrate the decorative side of life; but I have tried to remain amphibious. It's all right as long as lungs can work in another air. The real alchemy is being able to turn gold back again into something else. That's the secret that most of your friends have forgotten.

LILY. Why do you call your republic a republic? It is a closed corporation.

SELDEN. It is not my republic; if it were, I should have a coup d' état and seat you on the throne.

LILY. Whereas, in reality, you think I can never even get my foot across the threshold? You despise my ambitions--you think them unworthy of me!

SELDEN. Well, isn't that a tribute? I think them quite worthy of most of the people who live by them.

LILY. But if you think they are what I should really enjoy, you must think my ambitions are good enough for me.

SELDEN. Ah, my dear Miss Bart, I am not divine Providence, to guarantee your enjoying the things you are trying to get!

LILY. Then the best you can say for me is, that after struggling to get them I probably shan't like them? What a miserable future you foresee for me!

SELDEN. Have you never foreseen it for yourself?

LILY. Often. But it looks so much darker when you show it to me! Why do you do this to me? Why do you make the things I have chosen seem hateful to me, if you have nothing to give me instead?

SELDEN. No, I have nothing to give you instead. If I had, it should be yours, you know. *(LILY drops her head into her hands and weeps, SELDEN takes her hands.)* Isn't it natural that I should try to belittle all the things I can't offer you?

LILY. But you belittle me, don't you, in being so sure they are the only things I care for?

SELDEN. But you do care for them, don't you? No wishing of mine can alter that.

LILY. For all your fine phrases you're really as great a coward as I am, for you wouldn't have made one of them if you hadn't been so sure of my answer.

SELDEN. I am not so sure of your answer; and I do you the justice to believe that you are not either.

LILY. Do you want to marry me?

SELDEN. No, I don't want to--but perhaps I should if you did!

LILY. That's what I told you--you're so sure of me that you can amuse yourself with experiments.

SELDEN. I am not making experiments; or if I am, it is not on you but on myself. I don't know what effect they are going to have on me--but if marrying you is one of them, I will take the risk.

LILY. It would be a great risk, certainly--I have never concealed from you how great.

SELDEN. Ah, it's you who are the coward!

LILY. I shall look hideous in dowdy clothes; but I can trim my own hats. *(LILY stands up, SELDEN takes her hands and she leans against him. They stay like this for a moment. A dinner gong/train gong heard in the distance.)* I had no idea it was so late, and I've missed my appointment with Percy Gryce. We shall not be back in time for luncheon. Let us go. *(SELDEN is taken aback by her swift change of mood. He slowly takes out his cigarettes, lights one, and then offers one to LILY. She takes it and as he lights it for her she smiles at him.)* Were you serious?

(LILY looks at him quizzically.)

SELDEN. Why not? You see I took no risks in being so. *(LILY is taken aback by his retort.)* Come on, I have a train to catch.

(Sound of a train whistle.)

JUDY. When I think of what we've all done for Lily, I feel quite angry with her. The lengths I went to, to get her together with Percy—

GERTY. You never understood her. None of you. If you had she wouldn't be lying here in her coffin.

JUDY. Never understood her! How dare you say that. I did everything I could to help her. We all did, everybody played fair.

CARRY. The trouble with Lily was that she worked like a slave preparing the ground and sowing her seed; but the day she ought to have been reaping the harvest she overslept and went off on a picnic.

JUDY. Exactly! That was Lily all over. Why she behaved as though she had just discovered you, Lawrence, is beyond me. I warned her not to make an enemy of Bertha. I knew Bertha would poison Percy against her, given half a chance.

BERTHA. I don't know what you mean. It was my duty to tell Percy what he was letting himself in for, wasn't it, Percy?

PERCY. *(Embarrassed.)* Oh yes, Mrs Dorset. I was most grateful to you.

GERTY. You were grateful to be told a lot of lies--or half-truths?

PERCY. They weren't lies. I was already upset to find out that Miss Bart gambled. Do you know, I had never seen a girl play cards for money before. I was really quite shocked. Then

Mrs. Dorset told me about some Italian prince and an English aristocrat that Miss Bart had been involved with.

JUDY. And no doubt she told you about her borrowing money from Ned Van Alstyne to pay her gambling debts.

PERCY. Well, yes, she did mention it.

BERTHA. Carry told me about that, didn't you, Carry?

CARRY. I really can't remember, it's so long ago.

GERTY. But Ned Van Alstyne was a cousin of Lily's, and I happen to know she paid him back.

JUDY. I don't suppose, Bertha, you remembered to tell Percy that part of the story. Anyway, you knew your man, you knew just what to tell him to frighten him off.

PERCY. I do wish you wouldn't speak of me as though I weren't here. I was dazzled by Miss Bart, I don't deny it, but she broke all her promises to me--it was very disappointing, and she knew so much about Americana, I really thought... *(SELDEN laughs ironically.)* Oh, well, my mother had always warned me about such girls.

GERTY. Such girls! She was worth more than all of you put together. Her only crime was to try and live as one of you-- but she never had any money.

(LILY takes her hat off slowly and looks in the mirror. GUS stands behind her.)

GUS. Why such a worried look?

(LILY turns round quickly and gives him one of her dazzling smiles.)

LILY. Oh, Gus, I'm so glad you're here. Judy is angry with

me, and I want you to make my peace.

GUS. Oh, come now, that's nonsense, you know she's devoted to you.

LILY. She has set her heart on my marrying a great deal of money.

GUS. You don't mean Gryce?

LILY. Yes.

GUS. Good Lord--*Gryce*! Did Judy really think you could bring yourself to marry that portentous little ass?

LILY. I knew you'd understand me, Gus--I—

GUS. You bet I do. I could have told her you'd never put up with that milk-sop! Take my advice, Lily. Stay as you are until the right man comes along.

LILY. If only I could. But you see Judy's right--I *must* marry.

GUS. Must marry? Why?

LILY. I am in debt. I can't afford to go on living as all the women in my set do. My aunt gives me a small allowance, but I've lost money gambling lately, and I daren't tell her I have a pile of unpaid bills in my room.

GUS. It's confoundedly mean of your aunt to keep you so close.

LILY. She doesn't realize how things have changed. I will have to give up my way of life, there's nothing else I can do.

GUS. Have you no income of your own?

LILY. A tiny one. I wish I had someone like you to advise me on how to invest it. It seems to bring in less every year, but I know so little of money matters. Oh, I didn't mean to bore you with all this, but I want you to explain to Judy why I can't stay any longer, or be part of your set any more.

GUS. Look here, Lily. Will you let me do a turn for you?

LILY. A turn? What's that?

GUS. Pull off a little cash for you.

LILY. Oh, Gus I...

GUS. Trust me, Lily, I know what I'm doing. I can make things all right for you.

LILY. You're so good to me, Gus.

GUS. I don't want to see any more little worry lines on your face. *(He touches her face and she tries not to draw away.)* Hold out your purse. *(He takes his wallet out of his pocket. LILY backs away from him.)* Don't look so startled--this is a little advance...

LILY. No, I can't take it, I really...

GUS. It's a loan, Lily, on your first dividend.

LILY. *(LILY looks at the notes in his hand.)* You're *sure* I can pay you back?

GUS. *(Stepping close up to her with a smile.)* I'm sure. *(He gives her the money and she puts it in her purse.)* But not a word of this to anyone. Not even Judy. You understand. If a deal of this kind gets talked about, it usually falls through. *(He hold out his hand to her and she tentatively puts hers in his. He kisses it.)* To a successful partnership.

BERTHA. Was it true that Lily borrowed money from Gus?

JUDY. I don't think, under the circumstances, that you are in a position to ask me such a question.

BERTHA. What do you mean?

JUDY. Was it true that George asked Lily to marry him?

BERTHA. Of course not! What on earth gave you that idea?

JUDY. You see, you shouldn't listen to gossip.

GEORGE. *(Changing the subject.)* I'm starving. But I can't risk eating anything here. I might be poisoned.

BERTHA. Oh, indeed you might, dear. Do you remember Jack and Gwen's wedding reception? *Mousse* of lobster with champagne sauce.

GEORGE. Please--don't remind me.

GERTY. I wouldn't have missed their wedding for anything. It was beautifully done. I had never seen Lily looking so lovely. Do you remember, Lawrence?

GUS. Stunner, was the word I used.

JUDY. What are you talking about, Gus?

GUS. Lily. She looked a stunner. There was no one at that wedding to touch her.

(BERTHA and JUDY react.)

ROSEDALE. *(Looking at SELDEN.)* She was wearing the latest creation of the dress-maker she went to see at the Benedick.

BERTHA. *(Pointedly.)* I didn't know there were any dress-makers at the Benedick.

GERTY. I remember the diamond pendant you gave them, Mr. Rosedale, it was as big as a dinner plate. And the exquisite white sapphire from you, Mr. Gryce.

BERTHA. That was the day you announced your own engagement, wasn't it, Percy?

GERTY. I ran in for a minute to tell Mrs. Peniston about the wedding. She nearly fainted when I told her they served melons before the *consommé*.

JULY. I didn't care much for the bridesmaids' dresses. They certainly didn't look the three hundred dollars apiece they are supposed to have cost.

CARRY. I must say I was glad Lily decided not to be a bridesmaid; that shade of salmon-pink wouldn't have suited her.

BERTHA. That wasn't the only reason; the truth was she had attended too many brides to the altar, and...

GERTY. Mrs. Peniston wanted to know everything-- whether the old Van Osburgh Sèvres was used at the bride's table, what color Mrs. Van Osburgh's gown was, what everyone was wearing. She had been told that you were the best dressed person there, Mrs. Dorset.

JUDY. I've no doubt your dress *did* cost more than anyone else's.

BERTHA. I went to that new man in Paris. I had to spend a day with him at his villa in Neuilly, before he would take my order!

CARRY. I never saw you looking better, you were in tremendous spirits that day.

JUDY. Of course you were. You'd made the match between Evie and Percy, and got your revenge on Lily. Mind you, Maria Van Osburgh was in seventh heaven, she had almost despaired of marrying Evie, in spite of her fortune.

PERCY. I hope you're not suggesting I married Evie for her money--I already have a...

GUS. Ignore them, Percy. It's just women's talk! By the way, Rosedale, you promised me more information on the Ridenour deal. My luck has not been so great lately, and I could do with a good "turn".

ROSEDALE. Ask Welly Bry, why don't you? He can't put a foot wrong at the moment.

JUDY. I will never get used to the Wellington Bry's meteoric rise in society.

CARRY. You are such a snob, Judy! Don't forget they had the benefit of my guidance and expertise.

JUDY. That doesn't alter the fact that Louisa Bry's background is somewhat obscure. You get paid for your guidance and expertise, but my life is too busy to spend valuable time breaking in "new" people.

CARRY. You must admit though, she does things well. I remember telling her that a good cook was her best introduction to society.

BERTHA. Not to mention buying a house on Fifth Avenue.

JUDY. That cross between an Italian pleasure hall and the Trianon, you mean!

PERCY. Yes, yes! That's just how my mother describes it. She misses her visits with Mrs. Peniston. That was how she kept up with all the gossip. Mrs. Peniston knew everything that was going on.

GERTY. I remember sitting with her once. She was peering through her binoculars and keeping up a running commentary. "There's the Van Osburgh carriage on the way to the opera. *(MUSIC from La Traviata very softly in background.)* Grace tells me their last ball was exceedingly dull. Not that she was invited, of course, but she hears all the gossip and passes it on to me".

PERCY. Talking of gossip, Simon Rosedale has doubled his money, you know! Only he and Welly Bry seem to have found the secret of making money on Wall Street last winter, when everyone else was losing theirs.

GEORGE. How else could he have bought the Greiner's house on Fifth Avenue?

BERTHA. And everything else that goes with it!

ROSEDALE. Miss Lily, will you allow me to take you to the opening night of the opera season? I have my own box, you know. Mrs. Fisher and the Dorsets are coming, and I've secured a tremendous admirer of yours, who'll never forgive me if you don't accept. *(LILY remains silent.)* Gus Trenor has promised to come to town on purpose. I fancy he'd go a good deal farther for the pleasure of seeing you.

(ROSEDALE hands LILY some opera glasses.)

LILY. *(Looking around the auditorium through the opera glasses.)* The Trenors are my best friends--I think we should all go a long way to see each other.

ROSEDALE. Well, I wasn't thinking of Mrs. Trenor at the moment--they say Gus doesn't always, you know. By the way, how's your luck been going on Wall Street. I hear Gus pulled off a nice little pile for you last month.

LILY. I had a little bit of money to invest, and Mr. Trenor advised my putting it in stocks instead of a mortgage. I made a lucky "turn" as you call it. You make a great many yourself, I believe.

(GUS enters box and ROSEDALE leaves.)

GUS. Look here, Lily, I've hardly laid eyes on you for the last month. How is a fellow ever to see anything of you? I'm in town three or four days a week, but you don't seem to remember my existence nowadays unless you want a tip out of me. Why can't we go off somewhere on a little lark together? The plain English of it is that, now you've got what you wanted out of me, you'd rather have any other fellow about.

(GUS swigs a tot of whiskey from a hip flask.)

LILY. Don't be foolish, Gus; I can't let you talk to me in that ridiculous way. If you really want to see me, why shouldn't we take a walk in the park one afternoon?

GUS. All right, then: that's a go.

(GUS leaves the box as GEORGE enters.)

GEORGE. I wish Gus would draw the curtain when he leaves the box. The draughts are damnable. Well, here we are, Lily, in for another six months of operatic caterwauling. Bertha puts me through a course of this every winter. It isn't so bad on Italian nights--then she comes late, and there's time to digest. But when they give Wagner we have to rush dinner and I pay up for it. Lily, Bertha wants you to come down to our place next Sunday. That silly ass Silverton is bringing a lot of intellectual bores with him--Bertha and he are getting tremendously thick. Do for heaven's sake say yes--for my sake.

LILY. George, I'd love to. What an exciting week it will be. You're coming to the Welly Brys' aren't you?

(MUSIC changes to quartet. "Valse Bluette", Ricardo Drigo.)

(ON SCREEN. Invitation. Mr. and Mrs. Wellington Bry request the pleasure of your company at a "Tableaux Vivants" on Wednesday, December 3rd, 1903 at 5pm, followed by a buffet supper.)

CARRY. I remember suggesting that *tableaux vivants* and expensive music were the most likely baits to attract the desired prey.

BERTHA. You made quite a coup persuading all those fashionable women to exhibit themselves and Paul Morpeth to organize it. It was he who suggested I portray Titian's daughter, do you remember?

(BERTHA takes up the pose from the painting.)

CARRY. As if we could ever forget it! And I was...
GUS. Dona Isabel de Porcel. Francisco de Goya.

*(CARRY strikes the pose. They ALL clap. During this exchange
LILY is getting ready for her tableau.)*

ROSEDALE. How splendid Miss Smedden from Brook-
lyn looked! She showed the sumptuous curves to perfection.
GEORGE. I preferred Mrs. Van Alstyne's frailer Dutch type.
GERTY. Wasn't it dear of Lily to get me that invitation? Of
course it would never have occurred to you, Carry, to put me
on the list, and I should have been so sorry to miss seeing it
all. That ballroom! Some one told me the ceiling was by
Veronese--you would know, of course, Lawrence. I suppose it
was very beautiful, but his women were so dreadfully fat.
SELDEN. They were goddesses, Gerty.
GERTY. I can only say that if they'd been mortals and had
to wear corsets, it would have been better for them. I think our
women are much handsomer. *(MUSIC gets louder.)* Did you
ever see such jewels? Lily wouldn't tell me what she's appear-
ing as. She said it was a secret. Oh, Lawrence, I'm so excited.
GUS. How much longer do we have to wait for Miss Bart
to appear?
CARRY. Not much longer now. Then we can all go to supper.
ROSEDALE. Staying for supper, Gus?
GUS. Not if I know it! When people crowd their rooms so
that you can't get near anyone you want to speak to, I'd as
soon sup in the elevated in the rush hour. My wife was dead
right to stay away. Life *is* too short to spend it breaking in
"new" people.

(MUSIC changes. "Poème", Zdenek Fibich. Lighting changes.)

CARRY. Ladies and gentlemen, we now come to the last of the tableaux. Miss Lily Bart.

(A gasp is heard from the audience. Everyone stops talking as LILY is revealed as Joshua Reynolds's, Mrs. Lloyd. There is a general intake of breath and then silence. The moment is held before the applause starts.)

ROSEDALE. Gad, what a show of good-looking women. Not one of them could touch Lily though. I never knew until that night what an outline she had. There wasn't a break in the lines anywhere.

GUS. I suppose she wanted us to know it, too! It was a deuced bold thing to show herself in that get-up.

GEORGE. Damned bad taste, in my opinion.

ROSEDALE. How clever of her to select Joshua Reynolds's Mrs. Lloyd. It was as though she had stepped into the canvas, not out of it. She embodied Mrs. Lloyd, without ceasing to be herself. My God, if I could have got Paul Morpeth to paint her like that, the picture would've appreciated a hundred per cent in ten years.

GERTY. Wasn't she too beautiful, Lawrence? Didn't you like her best in that simple dress? It made her look like the real Lily--the Lily I knew.

SELDEN. The Lily *we* knew.

(LILY comes out of the tableau. She looks at SELDEN who is gazing into space. LILY starts to waltz on her own and after a few moments SELDEN takes her in his arms and

they dance together.)

LILY. You never speak to me--you think hard things of me.

SELDEN. I think of you at any rate, God knows!

LILY. Then why do we never see each other? We've not been alone since that morning at Bellomont. I have never recovered my self-respect since you showed me how poor and unimportant my ambitions were.

SELDEN. I thought, on the contrary, that I had been the means of proving they were more important to you than anything else.

LILY. Why can't we be friends? You promised once to help me.

SELDEN. The only way I can help you is by loving you.

(They stop dancing and look at each other. SELDEN kisses her. For a moment she leans against him and then draws away.)

LILY. Ah, love me, love me--but don't tell me so!

SELDEN. When may I come and see you?

LILY. Tomorrow, at four.

SELDEN. Tomorrow, at four.

(Tableau waltz. LILY melts away leaving SELDEN and GUS facing each other. SELDEN glares at GUS for a moment.)

GUS. Why are you looking at me like that, Selden?

(SELDEN turns away. GUS takes a swig from his flask.)

END OF ACT I

ACT II

(Act II starts exactly where Act I finished.)

GUS. Why are you looking at me like that, Selden? *(SELDEN turns away and GUS drinks quickly from his flask. Sound of doorbell. He sees LILY.)* Ah, Lily, come along in, you look a little pinched, I'll give you a nip of brandy to warm you up. It's not often you grace us with your company in New York.

(GUS hands LILY a drink and offers her a cigarette, which she takes and he lights for her.)

LILY. Thank you Gus. Where's Judy?

GUS. Judy?--Why, you see, Judy's got a devil of a head-ache--quite knocked out with it, poor thing--she asked me to explain--make it all right, you know--Come and sit down.

(GUS tries to take her hand, but she breaks free.)

LILY. Do you mean to say that Judy's not well enough to see me? Doesn't she want me to go upstairs? I'll only stay a minute.

(GUS drains his glass.)

GUS. The fact is, she's not up to seeing anybody. If she'd

known where you were dining she'd have sent word.

LILY. She did know where I was dining; I mentioned it in my note. But it doesn't matter, I'll come and see her in the morning.

GUS. Yes: exactly--that's capital. I'll tell her you'll pop in tomorrow morning. Now do sit down a minute, there's a dear, and let's have a nice quiet jaw together.

(GUS pours himself another drink.)

LILY. No, not tonight. It's too late. Please call a cab for me.

(GUS moves quickly to bar her exit.)

GUS. Why must you go, I should like to know? If Judy'd been here you'd have sat gossiping till all hours--you can't even give me five minutes!

LILY. That's rather different, isn't it?

GUS. Yes, it's always different where I'm concerned! I couldn't get near you tonight--I went to that damned vulgar party just to see you, and there was everybody talking about you. I tried to come up and say a word--you never took any notice.

LILY. Don't be absurd, Gus. It's past eleven, and I must really ask you to ring for a cab.

GUS. And supposing I won't ring for one--what'll you do then?

LILY. I shall go upstairs to Judy.

(GUS lays his hand on LILY'S arm.)

GUS. Look here, Lily: won't you give me five minutes?

LILY. Not tonight, Gus: you—

GUS. Very well, then: I'll take 'em. And as many more as I want. Go and sit down there, please: I've got a word to say to you.

LILY. You must say it another time. I shall go up to July unless you call a cab for me at once.

GUS. Go upstairs and welcome, my dear; but you won't find Judy. She ain't there. She's at Bellomont.

LILY. Nonsense--I don't believe you. I am going upstairs. If she hadn't come she would have sent me word—

GUS. She did; she telephoned me this afternoon to let you know.

LILY. I received no message.

GUS. I didn't send any.

LILY. I can't imagine your object in playing such a stupid trick on me; but if you have fully gratified your peculiar sense of humor I must again ask you to send for a cab.

GUS. Look here, Lily, don't take that high and mighty tone with me. I *did* play a trick on you; I own up to it; I tried to tell you at the Brys', but you were too busy being made a fuss of. If you think I'm ashamed you're mistaken. Lord knows I've been patient enough--I've hung around and looked like an ass. And all the while you were letting a lot of other fellows make up to you... but you'll know better now. That's what you're here for tonight. I've been waiting for a quiet time to talk things over, and now I've got it I mean to make you hear me out.

LILY. I don't understand what you want.

GUS. I'll tell you what I want: I want to know just where you and I stand. Hang it, the man who pays for the dinner is generally allowed to have a seat at the table.

LILY. I don't know what you mean--but you must see, Gus, that I can't stay here talking to you at this hour—

GUS. Gad, you go to men's houses fast enough in broad daylight--strikes me you're not always so deuced careful of appearances.

LILY. If you have brought me here to insult me—

GUS. Don't talk stage-rot. I don't want to insult you. But a man's got his feelings--and you've played with mine too long. I don't grudge the money--or double the money—

(GUS goes towards LILY.)

LILY. The money? What money? *(Pause.)* Do I owe you money?

GUS. I'm not asking for payment in kind. But there's such a thing as fair play--and interest on one's money--and hang me if I've had as much as a look from you—

LILY. Your money? What have I to do with your money? You advised me how to invest mine... you must have seen I knew nothing of business... you told me it was all right—

GUS. It *was* all right--it is, Lily; you're welcome to all of it, and ten times more. All I want is a word of thanks from you.

LILY. I *have* thanked you; I've shown I was grateful.

GUS. It's not the money--there's plenty where that came from--you can have as much as you want.

LILY. *(Slowly with horror.)* It was *your* money then--not mine?

GUS. Yours?

LILY. You told me you'd made it for me. You said you had a way of doubling my little investments.

GUS. So I had. All the women know what that means.

LILY. And you thought I knew? Oh, the shame of it!

GUS. Lily--look here--don't take it this way. *(He lays his hand on her arm.)* If you'd only be a little kind to me--I am mad about you.

LILY. Don't touch me! If I owe you money you shall be paid in full.

GUS. Ah--you'll borrow from Selden or Rosedale--and take your chances of fooling them as you've fooled me!

LILY. I tell you, you shall have back every penny.

GUS. Do you suppose that's the kind of interest a man's after when he spends money on a pretty woman? By Gad, Lily, you've fooled me too long! I didn't begin this business, you know. I kept out of the way, and left the track clear for the other chaps, till you rummaged me out and set to work to make an ass of me--an easy job you had of it, too. That's the trouble--it was too easy--and you got reckless. Thought you could turn me inside out, and chuck me into the gutter like an empty purse--but that ain't playing fair--that's dodging the rules of the game. I know I'm not talking the way a man is supposed to talk to a girl, but hang it--there's not time to choose my words. You've never let me have a minute alone with you—

(GUS seizes LILY'S hand. Furies--COMPANY--start to gather. LILY, trying to control her panic, finally confronts him with a clear look.)

LILY. Well, I'm alone with you now. Have you anything more to say?

GUS. Lily--go home! Go away from here.

(LILY runs up the stairs. SELDEN sees her leaving GUS'S house. The Furies start pursuing her. Furies MUSIC starts very softly building throughout the scene.)

SELDEN. *(Very angry.)* I saw her leaving your house that night, Trenor. What did you say to her? What did you do to her?

GUS. I don't know what you are talking about, Selden. *(Takes another swig from his flask.)* She had come to see Judy, there was nothing wrong in that.

SELDEN. You're lying, Trenor. You told me yourself at the club, that Judy had cancelled her trip to town. You ruined her reputation, it's you who brought her to this. It's all your fault, Trenor.

JUDY. Lily knew perfectly well I was at Bellomont. She just wanted to get some more money out of Gus.

SELDEN. You tricked her into that meeting with you. You're trying to make up for it now, by taking her to Bellomont, but it's all show. You just used her and then cast her aside--all of you!

GUS. How dare you speak to me like that.

(The COMPANY join in gradually, building to a crescendo. LILY stands watching and listening with growing horror. They begin to take on the shape of the Furies by swinging their capes and coats. LILY rushes among them.)

GEORGE. When a girl's as good-looking as that she'd better marry and then no questions are asked.

CARRY. She could have married--more than once--but whenever the opportunity presented itself she always shrank from it.

GEORGE. There is no provision as yet, in our society, for a young woman who claims the privileges of marriage without assuming its obligations.

GUS. She stood there as if she were up for auction. That Town Talk column in the paper was full of her the next day.

BERTHA. I'm not surprised. Flaunting herself in that flimsy dress. What else did she expect?

(The MUSIC reaches a crescendo. LILY screams out.)

LILY. Gerty! Gerty!

GERTY. Lily--what is it?

LILY. Gerty, the Furies... you know the noise of their wings-- alone, at night, in the dark? But you don't know--there is nothing to make the dark dreadful to you--the Furies may sleep, but they are there, always there in the dark corners. I can hear the clang of their wings in my brain. Tomorrow at four--he's coming tomorrow at four.

(GERTY helps LILY get out of her tableau costume and into another dress.)

GERTY. Listen, Lily--try and tell me what happened, it will clear your poor head. You were dining at Carry Fisher's. Lawrence went to find you there--actually, he had promised to have supper with *me* after the tableau. I had spent all day preparing...

LILY. *(She lets out a sob.)* He went to find me? And I missed him! Oh, Gerty, he tried to help me. He told me--warned me long ago--he foresaw that I should grow hateful to myself. Gerty, you know him--you understand him--tell me; if I went to him, if I told him everything--if I said: I am bad through and through--I want admiration, I want excitement, I want money--yes, *money!* That's my shame, Gerty--and it's known, it's said of me--it's what men think of me--If I said it all to him: I've sunk lower than the lowest, for I've taken what they take, and not paid as they pay--oh, Gerty, you know him, you can speak for him: if I told him everything, would he loathe me? Or would he pity me, and understand me, and save me from loathing myself?

GERTY. *(Pauses and then very quietly speaks.)* Yes: I know him; he will help you.

(Clock strikes four.)

LILY. Four o'clock. *(Tableau MUSIC starts very softly. She gets a tea tray. Puts it down on the table.)* Ah, love me, love me, but don't tell me so. *(Door bell rings. LILY picks up a cup and saucer, expecting SELDEN. ROSEDALE enters.)* Oh! Mr. Rosedale.

(LILY pours tea.)

ROSEDALE. Miss Bart. Forgive me for calling unexpectedly, but when I saw you at the Brys' last night, in that plain white dress, looking as though you had a crown on, I said to myself: "By gad, if she had one she'd wear it as if it grew on her". I want a woman who will hold her head higher the more diamonds I put on it. *(LILY hands him the tea.)* I have more money than I know how to invest. What I want is the right woman to spend it. *(He sips his tea and looks at LILY attentively.)* I guess you know the lady I've got in view, Miss Bart.

LILY. If you mean me, Mr. Rosedale, I am very grateful--very much--flattered; but I don't know what I've ever done to make you think—

ROSEDALE. Oh, if you mean you're not in love with me, I've got sense enough to see that. And I ain't talking to you as if you were. I'm confoundedly gone on you, and I'm just giving you a plain business statement of the consequences. You're not very fond of me--*yet*--but you're fond of luxury, and style, and amusement, and of not having to worry about cash. You like to have a good time, and not to have to settle for it; and what I propose to do is to provide for the good time and do the settling.

LILY. *(She gives ROSEDALE a chilling smile.)* You are mistaken in one point, Mr. Rosedale: whatever I enjoy I am prepared to settle for.

ROSEDALE. I didn't mean to give offense; excuse me if I spoke too plainly. But why ain't you straight with me? You know there've been times when you were bothered--damned bothered--and as a girl gets older, the things she wants are liable to move past her and not come back. You've had a taste of bothers that a girl like you ought never to have known about, and what I'm offering you is the chance to turn your back on them once and for all.

LILY. You are quite right Mr. Rosedale. I *have* had bothers; and I am grateful to you for wanting to relieve me of them. It is not always easy to be quite independent and self-respecting when one is poor and lives among rich people; I have been careless about money, and I have worried about my bills. But I should be selfish and ungrateful if I made that a reason for accepting all you offer. You must give me time--time to think of your kindness--and of what I could give you in return for it.

(LILY rings the bell, holds out her hand with a charming gesture of dismissal. ROSEDALE rises and takes his leave. The clock chimes six times.)

LILY. *(Addressing SELDEN.)* **I was so afraid you would arrive while Rosedale was with me. After he'd gone, I waited and waited for you, still hoping you would come.** *(The COMPANY turn to look at the screen. LILY reads out loud from a newspaper that ROSEDALE has left on the table. ON SCREEN in newspaper print.)* **"Mr. Lawrence Selden was among the passengers sailing this afternoon for Havana and the West Indies on the Windward Liner Antilles."** *(She puts her head in her hands and sobs.)* **I understood then that you were never coming--that you'd gone away because you were afraid you might come.**

(The doorbell rings. LILY picks up a telegram. She tears it open with shaking hands and reads.)

LILY. Sailing unexpectedly tomorrow. Will you join us on a cruise of the Mediterranean? Bertha Dorset.

(Sunset. Sound of sea and seagulls. Roulette wheels. A brass-band playing the Meridian Waltz.)

SELDEN. Carry Fisher!
CARRY. Why, Mr. Selden! What a surprise!
SELDEN. Yes, isn't it! I had some legal business in Paris and it went better than I expected, so I decided to slip away to the south for a week.
CARRY. Are you staying in Monte Carlo?

SELDEN. No, I've made Nice my headquarters--I've just popped over for the day.

CARRY. Lily's in Monte, you know. She's been cruising the Mediterranean with the Dorsets. Have you seen her?

SELDEN. I met her briefly last night at the firework display in Nice with George Dorset and other admirers. How is Miss Bart?

CARRY. She's been a tremendous success here. Everyone adores her. There are rumors though that Bertha is quite put out by her popularity, and I shouldn't wonder if there's a storm brewing.

GEORGE. Have you seen Bertha?

LILY. No--when I left the yacht she was not yet up.

GEORGE. Do you know what time she and Ned came aboard? This morning at seven!

LILY. What happened?

GEORGE They missed the train after the fireworks in Nice--all the trains--they had to drive back.

LILY. Well—?

GEORGE. Well, they couldn't get a carriage at once, and when they did, it was a one-horse cab, and the horse was lame.

LILY. How tiresome! I'm so sorry--ought we to have waited?

GEORGE. The cab would scarcely have carried the four of us.

LILY. We should have had to walk by turn.s. It would have been jolly to see the sunrise.

GEORGE. Yes: the sunrise *was* jolly.

LILY. You saw it then?

GEORGE. I waited up for them.

LILY. Why didn't you call on me to share your vigil?

GEORGE. I don't think you would have cared for its *dénouement.*

LILY. Isn't that too big a word for such a small incident? The worst of it is the fatigue which Bertha has probably slept off by now.

(GEORGE collapses down onto a seat and puts his head in his hands and sobs.)

LILY. Now George! What are you going to do?

GEORGE. I can go to an hotel. I can telegraph my lawyers. By Jove, Selden's at Nice--I'll send for Selden!

LILY. No, no, *no!*

GEORGE. Why not? He's a lawyer, isn't he? One will do as well as another in a case like this.

LILY. As badly as another, you mean. I thought you relied on *me* to help you.

GEORGE. You do--by being so sweet and patient with me. If it hadn't been for you I'd have ended the thing long ago. But now it's got to end. You can't want to see me ridiculous.

CARRY. Lily, I must speak to you. The man who was in the carriage with you and George on the way back from the fireworks--that horrid little Dabham who does "Society Notes from the Riviera"--has been dining with us at Nice. He's telling everybody that you and George came back alone from Nice after midnight.

LILY. Alone--? When he was with us? *(LILY laughs but is silenced by the gravity of CARRY'S look.)* We *did* come back alone--if that's so very dreadful. But whose fault was it? Bertha got bored with the fireworks, and went off early, promising to meet us at the station. We turned up on time, but she didn't--

she didn't turn up at all.

CARRY. Then how on earth did she get back?

LILY. In a one-horse cab! At any rate, I know she's safely on board, though I haven't yet seen her; but you see it was not my fault.

CARRY. Not your fault that Bertha didn't turn up? My poor child, if only you don't have to pay for it.

BERTHA. I suppose I ought to say good morning.

LILY. I tried to see you this morning, but you were not yet up.

BERTHA. No--I got to bed late. After we missed you at the station in Nice I thought we ought to wait for you till the last train.

LILY. You missed us?

BERTHA. Yes.

LILY. You waited for us at the station?

BERTHA. Yes.

LILY. But I thought you didn't get to the station till after the last train left!

BERTHA. Who told you that?

LILY. George.

BERTHA. Ah, is that George's version? Poor George--he was in no state to remember what I told him. He had one of his worst attacks this morning, and I packed him off to see the doctor. It's very bad for him to be worried, and whenever anything upsetting happens, it always brings on an attack.

LILY. Anything upsetting?

BERTHA. Yes--such as having you so conspicuously on his hands in the small hours. You know, my dear, you're rather a big responsibility in such a scandalous place after midnight.

LILY. Well, really--considering it was you who burdened him with the responsibility!

BERTHA. By not having the superhuman cleverness to discover you in that frightful rush for the train? Or the imagination to believe you would take it without us--you and he all alone--instead of waiting quietly in the station till we *did* manage to meet you?

LILY. No; by our simply all keeping together at Nice.

BERTHA. Keeping together? When it was you who seized the first opportunity to rush off with the Duchess and her friends? My dear Lily, you are not a child to be led by the hand!

LILY. No--nor to be lectured, Bertha, really.

BERTHA. Lecture you--I? Heaven forbid! I was merely trying to give you a friendly hint. But it's usually the other way round, isn't it? I'm expected to take hints, not to give them: I've positively lived on them all these last months.

LILY. Hints--from me to you?

BERTHA. Oh, negative ones merely--what not to be and to do and to see. And I think I've taken them with admiration. Only, my dear, if you'll let me say so, I didn't understand that one of my negative duties was not to warn you when you carried imprudence too far. *(She turns to the COMPANY, which has just been joined by SELDEN.)* Miss Bart is leaving now. She will not be returning to the yacht.

(GEORGE steps to his wife's side, white-faced with anger.)

GEORGE. Bertha!--Miss Bart... this is some misunderstanding... some mistake... How can she leave at this hour?

(LILY with admirable control extends her hand to her hostess.)

LILY. I am joining the Duchess early tomorrow, and it seems more sensible for me to stay at an hotel for the night. Dear Mr. Selden, you promised to see me ashore. *(She turns to SELDEN. Furies MUSIC.)* Do you know of a quiet hotel?

SELDEN. An hotel--*here*--that you can go to alone? It's not possible.

LILY. What is, then? It's too wet to sleep in the gardens. You see my change of plan was rather sudden—

SELDEN. Good God--if you'd listened to me!

LILY. But I have. You advised me to leave the yacht, and I've left it.

SELDEN. Lily!

LILY. Oh, not now. Please, Lawrence, help me.

SELDEN. You will do as I tell you then. You must trust me.

GEORGE. Miss Bart--you'll shake hands, won't you? I want to apologize--to ask you to forgive me for the miserable part I played—

LILY. Don't let us speak of it: I was very sorry for you.

GEORGE. I was deceived: abominably deceived—

LILY. You must see that I am not exactly the person with whom the subject can be discussed.

GEORGE. But can I at least appeal to your pity? I'm at the end of my tether.

LILY. I can't see how I can possibly be of any help to you.

GEORGE. You're the only person who knows. There wouldn't be a hint of publicity--nothing to connect you with the thing. All I need is to be able to say: I know this... and this... and this.

LILY. You're mistaken; I know nothing; I saw nothing--absolutely nothing.

CARRY. We all knew the real reason you had invited Lily to join you in the South of France was to keep George happy while you conducted your *amour* with Ned Silverton.

BERTHA. Carry!

CARRY. Well, it's true isn't it? I wish I could have changed places with Lily, I would have known just how to look after George. The trouble with Lily was that she wasn't clever enough to see what you were up to, Bertha. If she had been, she would have known just the right moment to take the bandages off George's eyes.

GERTY. It was cruel of you to turn Lily off the yacht, Mrs. Dorset--unjust.

BERTHA. She was trying to get George to divorce me and marry her.

JUDY. You did it to make him think you were jealous, I suppose.

GEORGE. Lily was so kind to me. She was such a glorious creature, so full of life.

GERTY. You never gave her a chance to clear herself. She should have told her story before you all judged her.

JUDY. What was her story?

SELDEN. I don't believe she knew it herself. She certainly hadn't prepared a version in advance, as you did, Bertha. It was easy to believe your story. The power of money, you see. Your social credit is based on an impregnable bank account.

(ON SCREEN. Newspaper print. Obituary. On June 10th 1904, suddenly, Grace Julia Peniston, widow of Herbert Peniston. The funeral will take place on June 14th at Trinity Church, Wall Street, at 2 pm.)

VO MRS. PENISTON. When I offered you a home, Lily,

I didn't undertake to pay your gambling debts--and I shall certainly not do anything to give the impression I countenance your behavior. I consider you are disgraced. Tell Jennings I will see no one this afternoon but Grace Stepney.

LILY *(Reciting from memory.)* ... to my niece Lily Bart I leave ten thousand dollars. The residue of my estate, $400,000, my property and possessions, except those aforementioned, I leave to my dear cousin and name-sake, Grace Julia Stepney. **It struck me as rather humorous that the ten thousand dollars my aunt had left me so nearly represented the amount I owed you, Gus. A debt I was more and more desperate to get free of. For the first time I felt utterly alone. I shouldn't have minded getting the money, you know. None of you would have quite dared to ignore me then; and even if you had, it wouldn't have mattered, because I should have been independent of you. But now, what was to become of me?**

GERTY. Grace Stepney had no right to all that money. Mrs. Peniston changed her will when she heard you had thrown Lily off the yacht, Mrs. Dorset. You were responsible for her being disinherited.

ROSEDALE. The truth about any girl is that once she's talked about she's done for.

(ROSEDALE takes out a cigar and lights it.)

LILY. Mr. Rosedale, I am ready to marry you whenever you wish.

ROSEDALE. My dear Miss Lily, I'm sorry if there's been any little misapprehension between us--but you made me feel my suit was so hopeless that I had really no intention of renewing it.

LILY. I have no one but myself to blame if I gave you the impression that my decision was final. I want at least to thank you for having once thought of me as you did.

ROSEDALE. Ain't we going to be good friends all the same?

LILY. You mean making love to me without asking me to marry you?

ROSEDALE. That's about the size of it. I'm more in love with you than ever, but if I married you now, I'd queer myself for good and all, and everything I've worked for all these years would be wasted.

LILY. I understand perfectly. A year ago I should have been of use to you, and now I should be an encumbrance.

ROSEDALE. Yes: that's exactly it. You know I don't believe those stories about you--I don't *want* to believe them. But they're there, and my not believing them ain't going to alter the situation.

LILY. If they are not true, doesn't *that* alter the situation?

ROSEDALE. In novels, maybe. But not in real life. Why don't you use those letters of Bertha Dorset's you bought last year?

LILY. What letters?

ROSEDALE. Don't play games with me. I'm the owner of the Benedick--remember? I know how completely she's in your power.

LILY. I don't know what you are talking about.

ROSEDALE. Bertha Dorset's love letters to Lawrence Selden. Show her that you're as powerful as she is, and I will back you, and with my backing behind you, you'll keep her just where you want her to be. That's what I'm offering you. Don't run away with the idea that you can do it without me.

You can't. In six months you'd be back among your old worries, or worse ones. I am ready to lift you out of them tomorrow. What do you say, Miss Lily?

LILY. You are mistaken, both in the facts and in what you infer from them.

ROSEDALE. Now what on earth does that mean? I thought we understood each other!

LILY. Ah, we do *now*.

ROSEDALE. I suppose it's because the letters are to *Selden*. Well, I'll be damned if I see what thanks you've got from him.

LILY. Your avoidance of me, Lawrence, wounded me deeply. I was very near to hating you then; yet the sound of your voice, the way the light fell on your dark hair, the way you sat and moved and wore your clothes--even these trivial things were inwoven with my deepest life. It was bad enough being rejected by my family and friends, but your disapproval was harder to take. Don't you see, Lawrence, I had to take up my usual life and go about among people? My old friends chose to believe the lies about me, so I had to make new ones.

CARRY. Well, you can't spend the summer in town. Why don't you put a few things in your trunk and come down to Long Island with me tonight? I am going to stay with the Sam Gormers, and I've got *carte blanche* to bring my friends down there.

LILY. But Carry, I don't know them.

CARRY. They don't know you either; but that doesn't make a rap of difference. They do things awfully well.

LILY. But Carry—

CARRY. Oh, I know they're not *your* particular set, but they're very good fun. They were getting on a good deal faster than the Brys, but decided the whole business bored them, so they've started a sort of continuous performance of their own, a kind of social Coney Island, where everybody is welcome who can make noise enough and doesn't put on airs. Bring two evening dresses with you, and your tennis things.

LILY. Carry, I don't know—

CARRY. Now don't stand there with your nose in the air, my dear--it will be a good deal better than a broiling Sunday in town.

GERTY. *(To CARRY.)* I was strongly opposed to Lily taking your place on the Alaska trip with the Gormers, last summer. The Gormers were not suitable companions for her. I offered to give up my visit to Lake George, and stay in town with her.

CARRY. I know you did. You're a trump, Gerty, worth all the rest of us put together. But, Lily was used to a little higher seasoning.

GUS. Well, she certainly got it with the Gormers.

(Laughter from JUDY, PERCY, BERTHA and CARRY.)

CARRY. She was doing very well with the Gormers, but you had to spoil it Bertha, turning Mattie Gormer against her with your nasty insinuations. You were afraid of her. That's why you spread your poison.

GEORGE. So *that* was why you took up with the Gormers. I thought it was out of character for you to be so neighborly, much less to make advances to anyone outside our set.

BERTHA. I was curious to see how the *new* people were spending their money. We couldn't exactly avoid them, since they turned up everywhere--hunt balls, the country-club, the

Horse Show--Mattie Gormer certainly seized on that occasion to display herself as well as her horses. *(They ALL laugh.)* It amused me, that's all.

GERTY. You could afford to be amused--but Lily was cheapening herself and we all stood by and watched. We all failed her, *all* of us.

SELDEN. Not you, Gerty.

GERTY. Yes, me too. I could have done more, but you see I hated her once. I wanted happiness too--wanted it as fiercely and unscrupulously as Lily did--but I had no power to attain it. What right had I to dream the dream of loveliness? A dull face invites a dull fate. There is no place in your society for an "unmarriageable" girl, with no money. I had to be content to stay on the outside, looking in. And I was content, life had seemed so simple and sufficient, and you were beginning to take more notice of me, Lawrence. Lily took away my only chance of happiness and I came face to face with the fact that I hated her.

(GERTY breaks down and sobs.)

LILY. Oh, Gerty, I wasn't meant to be good.

GERTY. You look horribly tired, Lily, are you ill?

LILY. I don't sleep at night.

GERTY. Since when?

LILY. I don't know--I can't remember. Do I look ill? Looking ill means looking ugly. Gerty, I'd rather know the truth: am I perfectly frightful?

GERTY. You're perfectly beautiful now, Lily: your eyes are shining, and your cheeks have grown so pink all of a sudden—

LILY. Ah, they were pale, then. Why don't you tell me frankly that I'm a wreck? My eyes are bright now because I'm so nervous--but in the mornings they look like lead. And I can see the lines coming in my face--the lines of worry and disappointment and failure! Every sleepless night leaves a new one--and how can I sleep, when I have such dreadful things to think about?

GERTY. Dreadful things--what things?

(GERTY extricates herself from LILY'S grip. LILY carries on speaking arapidly and confusedly.)

LILY. Poverty, for one--and I don't know any that's more dreadful. You think we live *on* the rich, rather than with them: and so we do, in a sense--but it's a privilege we have to pay for! We eat their dinners, and drink their wine, and smoke their cigarettes, and use their carriages and their opera-boxes and their private cars--yes, but there's a tax to pay on every one of those luxuries. The man pays it by big tips to the servants, by playing cards beyond his means, by flowers and presents--and--and--lots of other things that cost; the girl pays it by tips and cards too--oh, yes, I've had to take up bridge again--and by going to the best dress-makers, and having just the right dress for every occasion, and always keeping herself fresh and amusing! *(LILY closes her eyes for a moment. GERTY watches her intently.)* It doesn't sound very amusing, does it? And it isn't--I'm sick to death of it! And yet the thought of giving it all up nearly kills me--it's what keeps me awake at night. I can't go on in this way much longer, you know--I'm nearly at the end of my tether. What can I do--how on earth do I keep myself alive? *(LILY looks at her watch.)* It's late; I must be off--I have an appointment with Carry Fisher. She's arranged for me to see a Mrs. Hatch at the Emporium Hotel. Apparently she wants a kind of social secretary. I'm rather hard-up just for the moment, and if I could find something to do, it would tide me over till the legacy is paid. Don't look so worried, you dear thing, and don't think too much about the nonsense I've been talking.

(LILY kisses GERTY.)

SELDEN. I was shocked when I found out it was you who introduced Lily to Mrs. Hatch, Carry.

CARRY. I made it quite clear to her that I myself was un-acquainted with Mrs. Hatch. I was not Lily's keeper, and after all she was old enough to take care of herself. She needed a job. I was only trying to help.

ROSEDALE. But you must have been aware of that woman's shady reputation, and that the Emporium Hotel was a hot-bed of vice and indolence.

CARRY. You should know, Mr. Rosedale, better than any of us--after all you were quite a frequenter of the place once, weren't you? All I knew was, that she came from the West, had been divorced more than once--but *I* could hardly pass judgment on that fact--and had a great deal of money. She was, also, helpless and unplaced, and Lily was the ideal person to introduce her to society.

GUS. I stayed at the Emporium once. It was over-heated, over-upholstered, and over-fitted with mechanical appliances, while the comforts of civilized life were as hard to get as in a desert. I suppose your uncle's device for excluding fresh air was partly to blame for the stuffiness, Percy.

(The ALL laugh. PERCY looks embarrassed.)

BERTHA. Mrs. Hatch and her friends kept no definite hours, I am told. Night and day flowed into one another, while a succession of hangers-on paraded through her suite.

ROSEDALE. *(Pointedly.)* You mean like Freddie Van Osburgh and Ned Silverton?

BERTHA. I was actually thinking more of the throng of manicurists, beauty-doctors, hair-dressers...

JUDY. Although Mrs. Hatch's relationship to them sometimes made them indistinguishable from her other visitors, I believe. Poor Maria was distraught when she heard Freddie was so involved with Mrs. Hatch. What was he thinking of?

PERCY. He was completely under Ned's influence, and Mrs. Hatch was very alluring, I hear. You know Ned has never been very discriminating in his choice of women. *(BERTHA and CARRY react.)* Poor Freddie, he thought it was a way of escaping the official social routine.

GUS. What luck Rosedale and I were able to remove Freddie from Mrs. Hatch's clutches when we did. I reckon another week and he'd have married her.

GEORGE. By Jove, Percy! You were damn nearly related to the woman!

JUDY. I knew my instinct was right about Lily. You thought I was cruel to snub her, but I never really trusted her, and when I heard from Maria, about Freddie's involvement with Mrs. Hatch, well, who else could have been behind it?

ROSEDALE. You're wrong. Lily wasn't mixed up in that affair. It wasn't her style.

LILY. Mr. Selden, what a surprise! I wonder that you were

able to trace me here. What may I ask has inspired this search?

SELDEN. I wanted to see you.

LILY. You appear to have kept that desire under remarkable control.

SELDEN. You are to let me take you away from here.

LILY. And may I ask where you mean me to go?

SELDEN. To Gerty, in the first place; the essential thing is that it should be away from here.

LILY. I am very much obliged to you for taking such an interest in my plans; but I am quite contented where I am, and have no intention of leaving.

SELDEN. That simply means that you don't know where you are!

LILY. If you have come here to say disagreeable things about Mrs. Hatch—

SELDEN. It is only with your relation to Mrs. Hatch that I am concerned.

LILY. My relation to Mrs. Hatch is one I have no reason to be ashamed of. She has helped me to earn a living when my old friends were quite resigned to seeing me starve.

SELDEN. Nonsense! Starvation is not the only alternative. You know you can always find a home with Gerty till you are independent again.

LILY. You show such an intimate acquaintance with my affairs that I suppose you mean--till my aunt's legacy is paid.

SELDEN. I do mean that; Gerty told me of it.

LILY. But Gerty does not happen to know that I owe every penny of that legacy.

SELDEN. Good God.

LILY. Every penny of it, and more too, and you now perhaps see why I prefer to remain with Mrs. Hatch rather than take advantage of Gerty's kindness. I have no money left, except my small income, and I must earn something more to keep myself alive.

SELDEN. But with your income and Gerty's, you and she could surely contrive a life together which would put you beyond the need of having to support yourself. Gerty, I know, is eager to make such an arrangement, and would be quite happy in it—

LILY. But I should not. There are many reasons why it would not be kind to Gerty nor wise for myself. *(Pause.)* You will perhaps excuse me from giving you these reasons.

SELDEN. I have no claim to know them, no claim to offer any comment or suggestion beyond the one I have already made. And my right to make that is simply the universal right of a man to enlighten a woman when he sees her unconsciously placed in a false position.

LILY. I suppose that by a false position you mean one outside of what we call society; but you must remember that I had been excluded from those sacred precincts long before I met Mrs. Hatch. As far as I can see, there is very little difference in being inside or out, and I remember you once telling me that it was only those inside who took the difference seriously.

SELDEN. Mrs. Hatch's desire to be inside may put you in the position I call false.

LILY. I don't know why you imagine me to be situated as you describe; but as you always told me that the sole object of a bringing-up like mine was to teach a girl to get what she wants, why not assume that is precisely what I am doing?

SELDEN. I am not sure that I have ever called you a successful example of that kind of bringing-up.

LILY. Ah, wait a little longer--give me a little more time

before you decide! Don't give me up; I may still do credit to my training!

GEORGE. I suppose we should have done more to help her--but I really had no idea...

JUDY. She'd already had all she was getting from us. She flouted our friendship--and anyway she passed out of my milieu.

BERTHA. Lily got exactly what she deserved. She always had to go her own way. I knew she would come to a sticky end.

CARRY. What a pity she didn't make a success of working at Madame Regina's. After all the trouble I went to, too. She should have taken my advice and worked in the showroom, modelling the hats, instead of insisting on trying to make them.

BERTHA. Sewing on spangles was obviously not her forte.

GERTY. If you had helped her, she wouldn't have had to sew on spangles. You could have set her up in her own hat shop, Mrs. Trenor.

GUS. Lily, owning a hat shop!

BERTHA. She was never really one of our set anyway.

ROSEDALE. No! None of our set would live in a boarding house, in a neighborhood where the garbage is left lying in the street. That's where the beautiful Miss Bart ended her days. I know, because I took her there two months ago after bumping into her in the street. It was a damnable outrage her being in a place like that. *(To LILY.)* You can't go on living here--it's no place for you! Someone told me you were staying with Miss Farish.

LILY. No: I am boarding here. I have lived too long on my friends. Besides I have joined the working classes. I'm learning to be a milliner--at least I was. I have been out of work for a week.

ROSEDALE. Out of work? What a way to talk! The idea of you having to work--it's preposterous. Are you serious?

LILY. Perfectly serious. I'm obliged to work for my living.

ROSEDALE. Good Lord--*you*? But what for? I knew your aunt had turned you down: Mrs. Fisher told me about it. But I understood you got a legacy from her—

LILY. I got ten thousand dollars; but the legacy is not to be paid till next summer.

ROSEDALE. Look here: you could *borrow* on it any time you wanted.

LILY. No; for I owe it already.

ROSEDALE. Owe it? The whole ten thousand?

LILY. Every penny. I think Gus Trenor spoke to you once about having made money for me in stocks.

ROSEDALE. *(Embarrassed.)* I remember something of the kind.

LILY. He made about nine thousand dollars. It was incredibly stupid of me, but I thought he was speculating with my own money: but then I knew nothing of business. When I found out that he had *not* used my money--unfortunately I had already spent it. He meant it out of kindness, of course; but it was not the sort of obligation one could remain under, so my legacy will have to go to pay it back. That is the reason why I am trying to learn a trade.

(LILY delivers this speech very clearly, with pauses in between to make her points.)

ROSEDALE. But--if that's the case, it cleans you out altogether.

LILY. Altogether--yes.

ROSEDALE. Look here, Miss Lily, I'm going to Europe next week--and I can't leave you like this. I can't do it. I know it's none of my business--you've let me understand that often enough; but things are worse with you now than they have been before, and you must see that you've got to accept help from somebody. I'll lend you the money to pay Trenor.

LILY. But...

ROSEDALE. See here, don't take me up till I've finished. What I mean is, it'll be a plain business arrangement.

LILY. That is exactly what Gus Trenor proposed; I appreciate your kindness--but a business arrangement between us would in any case be impossible, because I have no security to give when my debt to Gus Trenor has been paid.

ROSEDALE. Then, for pity's sake, use the letters. If you'd only let me, I'd set you up over them all. I'd put you where you could wipe your feet on them.

(LILY puts her hands over her ears. Furies MUSIC.)

LILY. **I took no sleeping drops that night, but lay awake viewing my situation. I had never been heard in my own defense. I was innocent of the charge on which I had been found guilty--and all because of your jealousy and maliciousness, Bertha. More and more the Furies had taken on your shape, but safely locked away among my papers, I had the means of stopping their pursuit.** *(She takes the letters out of her bag and looks at them.)* **To save yourself, you hadn't hesitated to ruin my life with a lie; why should I hesitate to make use of your letters to Lawrence? I'd kept them all that time, and now I was going to use them.** *(Furies MUSIC fades.)* **I was sufficiently familiar with your** habits to know you could always be found at home after five. You might not be "at home" to such an unwelcome visitor, but I knew you would receive me when you got my note. I felt dizzy with lack of food and sleep when I set off. A rush of cold rain hit my face. I had no umbrella and was still half a mile from my destination, so decided to walk across Madison Avenue and take the electric car. As I turned into the side street, a vague memory stirred in me. It was down this street I had walked with you, Lawrence, that September day two years ago. It was strange to find myself passing your house on my way to confront Bertha with her letters to you. I had such a longing to see you. I paused on the pavement and saw a light in your window. I came to tell you that I was sorry for the way we parted--for what I said to you that day at Mrs. Hatch's. I wanted you to know that I left her immediately after I saw you.

SELDEN. Yes--yes; I know.

LILY. And that I did so because you told me to. Before you came I had already begun to see that it would be impossible to remain with her--for the reasons you gave me; but I wouldn't admit it--I wouldn't let you see that I understood what you meant.

SELDEN. Ah, I might have trusted you to find your own way out--don't overwhelm me with the sense of my officiousness!

LILY. It was not that--I was not ungrateful.

(LILY feels tears beginning to run down her cheeks.)

SELDEN. You are very tired. Why won't you sit down and let me make you comfortable? *(He draws LILY to a chair.)*

And now you must let me make you some tea: you know I always have that amount of hospitality at my command. *(LILY shakes her head as more tears roll down her face.)* You know I can coax the water to boil in five minutes.

LILY. No: I drink too much tea: I would rather sit quietly--I must go in a moment. *(SELDEN stands looking at LILY in silence. She is lost in her own thoughts. After a long pause, MUSIC. Very softly the Tableau Waltz.)* I must go. But I may not see you again for a long time, and I wanted to tell you I have never forgotten the things you said to me at Bellomont-- about **the republic of the spirit**--and that sometimes--sometimes when I seem farthest from remembering them--they have helped me, and kept me from mistakes; kept me from really becoming what many people have thought me.

SELDEN. I am glad to have you tell me that; but nothing I have said has really made any difference. The difference is in yourself--it will always be there. And since it *is* there, it can't really matter to you what people think.

LILY. Ah, don't say that--don't say that what you have told me has made no difference. It seems to shut me out--to leave me all alone with other people. *(She gets up, feeling stronger and looks SELDEN fully in the face.)* Once--twice--you gave me the chance to escape from my life, and I refused it; refused it because I was a coward. Afterward I saw my mistake--saw I could never be happy with what had contented me before. But it was too late; you had judged me--I understood. It was too late for happiness--but not too late to be helped by the thought of what I had missed. That is all I have lived on--don't take it from me now! Even in my worst moments it has been like a little light in the darkness. Some women are strong enough to be good by themselves, but I needed the help of your belief in me. Perhaps I might have resisted a *great* temptation, but the little ones would have pulled me down. And then I remembered--I remembered you saying that such a life could never satisfy me; and I was ashamed to admit to myself that it could. That is what you did for me--that is what I want to thank you for. I wanted to tell you that I have always remembered; and that I have tried--tried hard... *(She starts to cry again. She takes out her handkerchief and finds the packet of BERTHA'S letters in her pocket.)* I have tried hard--but life is difficult, and I am a very useless person. I can hardly be said to have an independent existence. I was just a screw or a cog in the great social machine I called life, and when I dropped out of it I found I was of no use anywhere else. After all, I was brought up to be ornamental. What can one do when one finds that one can only fit into one hole? One must get back to it or be thrown out into the rubbish heap--and you don't know what it's like in the rubbish heap!

(LILY attempts a smile.)

SELDEN. You have something to tell me--do you mean to marry?

LILY. You always told me I should come to it sooner or later!

SELDEN. And you have come to it now?

LILY. I shall have come to it--presently. But there is something else I must come to first. There is some one I must say goodbye to. Oh, not *you*--we are sure to see each other again--

but the Lily Bart you knew. I have kept her with me all this time, but now we are going to part, and I have brought her back to you--I am going to leave her here. When I go out presently she will not go with me. I shall like to think she has stayed with you--and she'll be no trouble, she'll take up no room. *(LILY goes towards SELDEN and holds out her hand.)* Will you let her stay with you?

(SELDEN catches LILY'S hand and holds it to him.)

SELDEN. Lily--can't I help you?

LILY. Do you remember what you said to me once? That you help me only by loving me? Well--you did love me for a moment; and it helped me. It has always helped me. But the moment has gone--it was I who let it go. And one must go on living. Goodbye.

(LILY lays her other hand on SELDEN'S and they stare intently at each other. SELDEN keeps hold of her hand.)

SELDEN. Lily, you musn't speak in this way. I can't let you go without knowing what you mean to do. Things may change--but they don't pass. You can never go out of my life.

LILY. No, I see that now. Let us always be friends. Then I shall feel safe, whatever happens.

SELDEN. Whatever happens? What do you mean? What is going to happen?

LILY. Nothing at present--except that I am very cold.

(LILY goes to a brazier.)

SELDEN. Oh, Gerty, how thin her hands looked while she stood in front of the fire; her figure seemed to have shrunk and the reflection from the flames intensified the shadows under her eyes. *(LILY takes the letters out of her pocket and puts them on the fire.)* I was aware that she drew something from her dress and dropped it in the fire. I stood there, unable to break the silence, and then she was gone. When I woke the next morning, everything seemed so clear. I knew without any doubt, what I had to say to Lily, and rushed off, full of joy to tell her—

ROSEDALE. What happened that night, Miss Farish?

GERTY. We're not absolutely sure. The doctor found a bottle of chloral.

ROSEDALE. She told me she had been sleeping badly for a long time.

GERTY. She must have taken an over-dose by mistake. There is not doubt of that, no doubt at all.

SELDEN. The doctor was very kind. Gerty and I went through her things.

GERTY. It didn't take long, there wasn't much to go through. I left Lawrence alone with her; that is what she would have wished.

(Very softly MUSIC on a saxophone starts playing. Far away the sound of a train.)

SELDEN. She had left everything so tidy. There were two letters on her desk. One to her bank, and the other to Augustus Trenor. She had received her legacy that day, there was a letter from the lawyer amongst her papers. I went through her check book and she had paid off all her debts, including the

$9000 she owed you, Gus. The obligation had become intolerable to her, she paid you back, knowing that she would face unmitigated poverty.

(Train in mid-distance.)

LILY. **There were in me two beings, one drawing deep breaths of freedom, the other gasping for air. As I lay in my bed, the horizon expanded, the air grew stronger, and the free spirit quivered for flight. I had the first glimpse of the central truth of existence, the continuity of life. I thought again of your "republic of the spirit", but this seemed something deeper and finer than that, and I wanted to tell you something, some word I had found that would make life clear between us. I was afraid of not remembering it when I woke. I knew that if I could only say it to you everything would be well.**

SELDEN. We had never really been at peace together--life always seemed to keep us apart--but at least I *had* loved her, and in the silence, when you left us alone, Gerty, there passed between us the word which made it all clear.

(Saxophone MUSIC getting a bit louder. Train arriving at station. Lots of smoke.)

GERTY. *(Touching SELDEN'S arm.)* Dear Lawrence. The train has arrived. It's time to go.

(Slow fade until only the lilies on the coffin are lit.)

END OF PLAY

ACT I

Coffin
Spray of lilies
Shoe-box
Luggage
Cigarettes
Cigars
Lighters
Parasols
Fans
Handbags/Reticules
Jeweled watch
Tea tray
Cups and saucers etc.
Cake
Gold cigarette case on pearl chain
Books
Clock
Mirrors
Newspapers
Bundle of letters tied up with string
Roulette wheel, chips, dolly
Pen and paper
Pile of correspondence
Dollar bills
Omar Khayyam volume
Wallet
Opera glasses
Hip flask

ACT II

Glasses and drinks
Tea tray, etc.
Small hand bell
Telegram
Handkerchief
Brazier

ACT I

Gottschalk's "Suis Moi"
Saxophone music
Gottschalk's "Manchega"
Station sounds, trains shunting, steam, brakes, etc.
Street noises, car hooters, hansom cabs, etc.
"Manchega" reprise
Station announcement
Steam
Train lurching
Sound of roulette wheel
Joseph Lanner's Vermählungs-Waltzer
Gottschalk's Polka in Bb
Joseph Lanner's Abendsterne
Voice overs
Church bells
Birds singing
Hymn singing
Dinner gong
Train whistle
Intro to "La Traviata"
Valse Bluette (Drigo)
Poème, the tableau waltz (Fibich)
Reprise of Poème

ACT II

Door bell
Furies music
Clock striking four o'clock
Poème
Clock striking six o'clock
Doorbell
Sea, seagulls, roulette wheels, etc.
Band playing "Meridian Waltz"
Furies music
Poème reprise
Saxophone music
Train noises

WHITE BUFFALO
Don Zolidis

Drama / 3m, 2f (plus chorus)/ Unit Set

Based on actual events, WHITE BUFFALO tells the story of the miracle birth of a white buffalo calf on a small farm in southern Wisconsin. When Carol Gelling discovers that one of the buffalo on her farm is born white in color, she thinks nothing more of it than a curiosity. Soon, however, she learns that this is the fulfillment of an ancient prophecy believed by the Sioux to bring peace on earth and unity to all mankind. Her little farm is quickly overwhelmed with religious pilgrims, bringing her into contact with a culture and faith that is wholly unfamiliar to her. When a mysterious businessman offers to buy the calf for two million dollars, Carol is thrown into doubt about whether to profit from the religious beliefs of others or to keep true to a spirituality she knows nothing about.

ANON
Kate Robin

Drama / 2m, 12f / Area

Anon. follows two couples as they cope with sexual addiction. Trip and Allison are young and healthy, but he's more interested in his abnormally large porn collection than in her. While they begin to work through both of their own sexual and relationship hang-ups, Trip's parents are stuck in the roles they've been carving out for years in their dysfunctional marriage. In between scenes with these four characters, 10 different women, members of a support group for those involved with individuals with sex addiction issues, tell their stories in monologues that are alternately funny and harrowing..

In addition to Anon., Robin's play What They Have was also commissioned by South Coast Repertory. Her plays have also been developed at Manhattan Theater Club, Playwrights Horizons, New York Theatre Workshop, The Eugene O'Neill Theater Center's National Playwrights Conference, JAW/West at Portland Center Stage and Ensemble Studio Theatre. Television and film credits include "Six Feet Under" (writer/supervising producer) and "Coming Soon." Robin received the 2003 Princess Grace Statuette for playwriting and is an alumna of New Dramatists.